"The matter is out of my hands. If the Princess of Mahendrapuri has arranged to meet me in private, I, as a mere guest, can only oblige." He shook with laughter even as he caressed her blushing cheek with his thumb.

Intelligent and courageous! As much as he was handsome and well-mannered. Was it any surprise that he had stolen her heart! Lifting a small fist, she hit him on his chest in response to his teasing. When he laughed some more, she buried her face in his chest, her face heating up even as her heart galloped as fast as Agni when he raced through the plains. She sighed deeply when she felt his caressing hand at the back of her head.

Devendra wasn't laughing any more as he held her body close to his chest, relishing the contrast as her soft curves fitted into his hard planes. He had to make her his, soon. Tugging at her hair to pull her face up to his, he said, "I would like to make you my wife, princess. Will you be mine?"

Hemangini looked up into his dear face, struck with wonder at the need and desire in his gaze before responding, "I would be honoured, Prince Devendra."

ABOUT THE AUTHOR

Sundari Venkatraman is an Indie Author who has 56 books to her credit. These books have consistently featured in the Top 100 Bestseller Lists on Amazon India, Amazon USA, Amazon UK, Amazon Canada and Amazon Australia in both romance as well as Asian Drama categories. Her latest hot romances have all been on #1 Bestseller slot in Amazon India for over a month.

The Passionate Princess, Book #1 of The Princess Series, is the author's first attempt at penning a historical romance. The eBook held the No. 1 position in the Historical Romance category on Amazon India for three whole months after release.

Even as a child, Sundari absolutely loved the 'lived happily ever after' syndrome and she grew up on a steady diet of fairy tales, Phantom comics and Mandrake comics. It was always about good triumphing over evil and a happy ending after the protagonists surmounted all unexpected obstacles.

Once she entered her teens, Sundari switched her loyalties from fairy tales to Mills & Boon. While she loved reading both of these, she kept visualising what would have happened if there were similar situations happening in India; to local heroes and heroines. And of course, the joy of vanquishing the ubiquitous evil villains! Her imagination soared and she happily ensconced herself in a rosy romantic cocoon for many years.

Then came the writing—a true bolt from the blue! And Sundari Venkatraman has never looked back.

AUTHOR'S NOTE

My Dear Reader,

Thank you so much for showing interest in reading my latest book, my first historical romance. I am truly excited with this one as it has been a long-standing dream to write romances set in the past.

Having said that, I would like to mention that I have not used any real characters from Indian history. All characters in this book are purely from my imagination as are the places, backgrounds, kingdoms et al. What I have used from history is the time period, my novel being set in mid-fifteenth century, from 1481-1485 AD.

I have done my best to research this period for the food they ate, the garments they wore, the habits they followed and the like. I have also done my best to keep the language as old as possible. Of course, writing a historical romance set in India in English, is in itself an anomaly, hence do forgive me for the liberties I have taken. I have tried to inculcate a few words in the Indian language that are used for clothes and jewellery and words like *madira*, meaning an intoxicating drink similar to wine, just to make the background more authentic to the reader.

I have to mention something relevant here. The women of medieval India were way bolder and more forthcoming. They also had a lot more freedom to do what they pleased and never lived their lives under the thumbs of men—not their fathers, not their brothers, not their husbands. And sex was not considered the repressed activity of modern India. But one thing was considered fundamental: that a man cannot make love to a woman without her consent, even if she was his wife.

I have also given a bit of description to the scenes so that one can visualise the story as one reads it.

This is the first book in The Princess Series. I hope you enjoy reading it and will be able to give me a brief and honest feedback on Amazon and Goodreads.

Yours faithfully,
Sundari Venkatraman

Books by Sundari Venkatraman

Standalone novels
The Malhotra Bride
Meghna
The Madras Affair
An Autograph for Anjali
Twin Torment
Finding Anya
Mr. Perfect
Man Friday
Her Prince Charming
Love in Agartha
Arjun's Penance
The Floundering Author
Once Bitten Twice Lucky
Ryan Finds a Bride
Tinder Loving Care
Shaan Gets Hitched
For Better or For Worse

Collection of shorts
Matches Made in Heaven
Tales of Sunshine

The Groom Series Trilogy
#1 Groomnapped
#2 Gobsmacked
#3 Grounded

Dashavatar (Indian Mythology)
Matsya: The First Avatar
Kurma: The Second Avatar
Varaha: The Third Avatar
Narasimha: The Fourth Avatar
Vamana: The Fifth Avatar
Parashurama: The Sixth Avatar

The Writer's Toolkit (Non-fiction)
Publishing Your Book on Amazon KDP

Marriages Made in India Series
#1 The Runaway Bridegroom
#2 Her Smitten Husband
#3 His Drunken Wife
#4 Her Secret Husband
#5 The Casanova's Wife
#6 Her Bohemian Husband

The Bansal Legacy Trilogy
#1 Simha International
#2 Rose Garden International
#3 Maharaja International

Written in the Stars Series
#1 Scorpio Superstar
#2 Leo's Desire
#3 Taurus Temptation
#4 Virgo's Krush

The Thakore Royals Trilogy
#1 The Marriage Predicament
#2 Tied in Knots
#3 The Wooing of the Shrew

Romantic Shorts
#1 *Chahti Hoon Tumhe*
#2 Beauty is but Skin Deep
#3 Madeinheaven.com
#4 An Arranged Match
#5 The Reluctant Bride
#6 *Shweta ka Swayamvar*
#7 Pappa's Girl
#8 Red Rose Dating Agency
#9 Rahat Mili
#10 Reema's Matchmakers
#11 The Matchmaker's Dream

**The Princess Series
(Historical Romance)**
#1 The Passionate Princess
#2 The Rebel Princess

The Passionate Princess

SUNDARI VENKATRAMAN

FLAMING SUN

Notion Press Media Pvt Ltd

No. 50, Chettiyar Agaram Main Road,
Vanagaram, Chennai, Tamil Nadu – 600 095

First published by Flaming Sun 2021
Printed & Distributed by Notion Press
Copyright © Sundari Venkatraman 2021
All Rights Reserved.

ISBN 979-8-88684-699-7

Cover design by: Unaiza Merchant
Beta read by: Lakshmi Ranganathan
Edited & marketed by: The Book Club

ACKNOWLEDGEMENT

Thank you so much Jayu and Lak for reading the story patiently, chapter by chapter and helping me with useful suggestions. Thank you Jayu for the research link and thank you Lak for coining the name Triumbaka for the *Kuldevi* of the Indrapuri royals.

Thank you so much Rubina Ramesh for your valuable suggestions. Thank you for *Rani Maa* and *Madira*.

CONTENTS

PROLOGUE

The Royal Astrologer

Indrapuri, 1483 AD

Queen Kanchana Devi waited in silence as she sat in her plush chair piled with cushions covered in silk, her calm demeanour laying lie to the agitated state of her mind. In front of her, some feet away, the royal astrologer Agnimitra was studying the horoscope of her daughter-in-law, Princess Hemangini.

Hemangini was married to Kanchana Devi's son, Devendra, the Crown Prince of Indrapuri. Fourteen months had passed after the wedding and until now there was no sight nor sound of a child in the imperial household of Indrapuri, a large kingdom set to the south of the Vindhya mountains.

The astrologer continued to study the horoscope in silence, marking something on the palm leaf that he had brought along with him. That the queen might be growing impatient didn't seem to bother the old man who had been working with the Indrapuri royals over the past two generations.

It was Astrologer Agnimitra who had predicted the birth of King Chandrabhan, insisting that it would be a boy. The king's father had gifted the royal astrologer a huge plot of land along with twenty cows and two bulls. This was besides the bag of hundred gold coins that he had been given.

Right now, Agnimitra looked at the horoscope of the crown princess, a deep frown drawing his thick eyebrows together. After some more time, he looked up at the queen and shook his head slowly from side to side. "I cannot tell you anything as of now, Your Majesty. The way Rahu and Ketu are positioned, I cannot see the chance of the princess becoming a mother, not in the near future. Maybe, if…" he paused, looking down at the horoscope to calculate some more.

The queen's face grew red with temper. Maybe it was time for the old astrologer to retire. How could he be so ambiguous in his prediction? Either Hemangini will become a mother or she will not. How could there be two ways about it?

"Agnimitra, will the princess bear a child or no?"

The astrologer's head went up in surprise at Queen Kanchana Devi's stern enquiry. Over the years, he had only been faced with the queen's gentleness and respect. This was something completely new. "Your Majesty! That's what I am trying to assess. Though I am rather confused about the positions of these two planets. I have never come across something like this before."

"What is your forecast? Will she have a child in the near future? Or no?" The proud queen had lost her patience by now and her voice veered towards a threat.

It was a good thing there was no one else in the room. Since the consultation was to be held in secret, the queen had ensured that all her maids were out. There was the one sentry stationed at the entrance to her chambers and he was too far away to be able to overhear the conversation. Agnimitra was sweating by now. Always having been treated with great respect by the noble family, he was not sure how to deal with the present situation. The queen had sent word for him in the absence of her husband, King Chandrabhan and son, Prince Devendra, who were taking a tour of the whole kingdom that stretched from the Godavari river in the north to the Tungabhadra river in the south. And fortunately, or unfortunately, Devendra's wife, Princess Hemangini, had also accompanied them.

Queen Kanchana Devi, who was keen to know when the kingdom would have an heir; had decided this was the ideal time to consult the royal astrologer regarding the same.

And that was the problem! For once in his life, the astrologer was unable to give an exact prediction. There was a possibility that Princess Hemangini would conceive. But that seemed to not be in the near future. The queen wanted to know if the princess would deliver the heir to the kingdom in the coming year.

He thought for a while before saying, "Your Majesty! As far as I can see, there is no reason that Princess Hemangini will not deliver a child. But it will take a long time." He was surprised to see the smile on the queen's face, before presuming that Kanchana Devi was happy that her daughter-in-law would definitely deliver the heir to the throne. It didn't strike him that his conclusion could be erroneous.

Relieved, he got up from his seat to bring both his hands together in a gesture of respect. "Will that be all, Your Majesty?"

"Yes, Agnimitra. Here! Take this!" She took a small bag containing ten gold coins and dropped it into his palms when he held them up to her. "You may go now."

When Agnimitra left, the queen's primary maid, Ratnamala, who had been keeping a watch from further down the corridor outside Kanchana Devi's chambers, quickly returned to the main hall of her mistress's rooms.

"Your Majesty!" She bent low in a gesture of respect before lifting her curious gaze to Kanchana Devi's face. "Is everything well?" The truth was that she was dying to know why the astrologer had visited the queen. Privy to every secret of Queen Kanchana Devi, the maid was rather disappointed that her mistress had not confided in her about the astrologer's visit.

The queen gave her maid a brilliant smile. "I think so. Why don't you massage my feet, Ratna? And I will tell you all about what I just found out."

Her disappointment wiped away with those words, the maid immediately went into the queen's adjacent dressing room to bring a small silver jar containing jasmine oil. "Would you like to lie down, Your Majesty?" she asked Kanchana Devi who was still seated in the grand chair.

Kanchana Devi shook her head. "I would rather be here, Ratna. Why don't you go and shut the door?"

The maid's glee knew no bounds as she almost flew to the doorway and instructed the sentry to shut the tall doors made of ornately carved wood before bolting the lock home. Rushing back to her mistress, she kneeled at her feet, removing the queen's anklets and toe rings made of gold embellished with precious stones. Placing a cushion on her own lap, she took the queen's right foot and held it against its softness as she looked eagerly at Kanchana Devi's face, waiting for her to speak.

"It appears that Hemangini is barren," declared the queen, a smirk on her face. It was a white lie, but the queen was not at all bothered about it. She was definitely going to make Princess Hemangini pay for garnering all of Prince Devendra's attention, so much so that he did not have much time left for his mother. That the princess was extremely beautiful and graceful only managed to fire Kanchana Devi's temper all the more. Her jealousy didn't spring from the fact that Devendra showered attention on his wife and not his mother. The truth was that the queen's husband, King Chandrabhan, had never showed her the same kind of love that her son had for his own wife.

"Hah!" Ratnamala's mouth opened wide as she stared at the queen, her mind racing. While she always kept the queen's secrets, it was the chief maid who spread all kinds of news—rumours at most times—in Indrapuri whenever required, at the behest of the majestic queen. Just now, she was dying to know if Kanchana Devi wanted this particular information known to people or not.

"What? Shouldn't you be upset that our great kingdom is going to be left without an heir?" Queen

Kanchana Devi gave her maid a mock glare, her lips in a pout.

"Your Majesty! Naturally, I am upset about it. But… but, I hope you will not mind if I ask you a question." Ratnamala continued to rub the queen's small feet with the fragrant jasmine oil as she uttered the words.

"What do you want to know?" The queen lifted a shapely eyebrow at her maid. At two and forty years, she was still a beautiful woman, though she had put on some weight over the past decade.

"I understand that it is only Princess Hemangini who is barren. What about our Prince? Prince Devendra must be able to become a father, won't he?" She gave her mistress a sly glance. Well aware of the haughty queen's dislike for her daughter-in-law, Ratnamala was only too happy to add fuel to that particular fire.

The queen threw back her head and laughed. "You, my Ratna, are extremely intelligent. No wonder you are the favourite amongst my maids." She quickly removed the twin-row of pearls with a diamond pendant that graced her neck and threw it at the maid who caught it deftly.

Grinning from ear to ear, Ratnamala bowed before the queen. "Thank you very much, Your Majesty. I am truly lucky to have your blessings!"

"You need to do something, Ratna."

"Anything you say, Your Majesty."

"This information is only between you and me, except for one other person."

"Who, Your Majesty?" Ratnamala asked eagerly. Oh, how she loved to spread gossip around! Especially something that was bound to create misery to others.

"Princess Hemangini's personal maid. You understand that she should never realise that the message came from me? It should be as if you are gossiping with her. Will you be able to do that?" The cunning queen gave her maid a shrewd glance. If there was anyone in the kingdom whom she could trust with such a task, it was Ratnamala.

A visibly excited Ratnamala nodded her head vigorously. "Leave it to me, Your Majesty! The task will be done."

The queen gave a sigh of pleasure. "Aah! Oh yes, Ratna. That's the exact spot. Do rub some more oil there." She leaned back against the cushion, her eyes shut and her face wreathed in smiles as she dreamed of the day when Hemangini would be completely out of her son's life.

Agnimitra stepped into his palanquin and sat down, ordering his men to take him back home. A deep frown on his face, he couldn't help wondering what the queen would do now. The fact of the matter was that he had not divulged the complete truth to her regarding Princess Hemangini's horoscope. The astrologer had not only studied the *Jyotish Shastra* deeply but had also read more than tens of thousands of horoscopes in his lifetime.

He was sure that Hemangini had never been with a man which was exactly the reason why she hadn't become pregnant. But then, she had been married to the Crown Prince of Indrapuri for fourteen months. How could this even be possible? Which is why he had not mentioned anything to the queen. Well, the astrologer knew the value of his head and body continuing to remain attached to one another.

The queen had not been in one of her better moods today. With the king absent from the capital city, Agnimitra had decided to take the safest route and given Kanchana Devi just enough information to keep her satisfied.

With a big sigh, he leaned back to shut his eyes, his fat body moving from left to right to match the rhythm of the palanquin as the bearers carried him home.

The Crown Prince
of Indrapuri

Mahendrapuri, 1481 AD

Prince Devendra galloped ahead of his men, his horse Vayu appearing to fly across the forest land, just as its name suggested. He had brought along ten men to the hunt and they had ridden for two days, camping at night around an open fire to keep the wild animals at bay. They hadn't come across any game during this time and he was sure they were not all that far away from the adjacent kingdom of Mahendrapuri.

It was only that morning they had come across a herd of deer. After rapidly striking down five spotted deer with his arrows, Devendra lost interest in the chase. After all, it was for food more than recreation that he had organised the hunt. His duty over, the prince was keen to explore the area beyond the forest, into the neighbouring kingdom of Mahendrapuri.

At twenty-two, Devendra was tall, almost seven feet, with strongly muscled shoulders to match. Well trained in archery, swashbuckling and wrestling, he was something of a one-man army. The prince was also a great orator and had the ability to sway crowds into his way of thinking without too much of an effort. From the day he was born, he had been trained to take over as the ruler of Indrapuri after his father, King Chandrabhan.

His mother, Queen Kanchana Devi, tended to cosset the prince, much to his chagrin. While he never defied her openly, he always breathed easier when not in her presence. As a child, he never could understand her behaviour. It was only later, when he turned sixteen, did the prince realise why his mother was the way she was.

Chandrabhan enjoyed women and while Kanchana Devi was his eldest consort, he had married three other women—Paromita, Suvarnarekha and Vaijayantimala—after her. Not satisfied with four wives, the king also maintained multiple mistresses in his harem.

Queen Paromita had two sons who were not much younger than Devendra. While Queen Suvarnarekha had given birth to a girl who was about ten now, Queen Vaijayantimala had made the king extremely thrilled when she gave birth to three offspring at the same time—two boys and a girl—and they were barely two years old.

Kanchana Devi was keen that her only child should be married soon and bring forth the heir to the next generation. Her worry was that one of Paromita's sons might get married first and his child would become the eldest of that generation. And to this end, she had been applying pressure on Prince Devendra.

But Devendra was not too sure about tying the knot with just any stranger. He enjoyed his women, but there were some things that he was clear about. He would marry the right woman at the right time. Once he had a wife, he would never look at another woman. The main reason for this was that he never wanted to be like his father who had hurt his mother deeply with his many wives and mistresses.

Except for this one quality, he adored his father. Just now, he rode his horse into Mahendrapuri which was much smaller than his own Indrapuri. It was to the west of his kingdom and was situated parallel to the seashore.

He stopped at the well where some women were drawing water. They giggled when they eyed the handsome man sitting astride the black horse with a white patch on its forehead. While his clothes were made of finely woven muslin, a *sarpech* of diamonds and emeralds graced the man's turban. Could he be a monarch?

One of the women stepped forward boldly to ask, "Who are you?"

With a gentle smile on his face, he replied, "I come from Indrapuri. It's a long way from here and both my horse and I are thirsty. Could you give us some water to drink?"

She looked at her friends before returning her gaze to him, giggling some more. "That is not the answer to the question I asked you. Who are you?"

He shrugged his broad shoulders before leaping down from his horse. "Will you know who I am if I give you my name?" he asked, walking towards her. Just as he expected, she stepped back before turning tail and rushing towards her friends. Laughing, he said, "I only need water and the direction to the royal palace, if you know the way, that is."

Could he be a messenger from Indrapuri? One of the women quickly offered a shining brass pot full of water for him to drink. Taking it in his hand, the prince asked, "May I have some for my horse?"

Another woman brought forth a wide clay vessel, placing it on the ground in front of the big horse which was at least seventeen hands tall. Another woman poured water into the vessel and watched on while the horse drank from it greedily.

"Thank you," said Devendra before drinking from the pot that he was still holding in his hand.

The women looked at each other, impressed by his behaviour. After all, he had insisted on quenching his horse's thirst before his own.

He returned the pot to the woman before getting back on his horse. "Which way is it to the Mahendrapuri palace?" he asked.

They pointed left and he took off, feeling refreshed. It wasn't long before he found himself in a garden that was lush with flowering shrubs. The whole area smelled divine while he could hear bees buzzing around the flowers that thrived in such brilliant colours. Getting down from his horse, he took the reins in his hand as he walked in the direction of a fountain which seemed to be in the centre of the beautiful garden.

Vayu stopped to nibble at the fresh grass beneath his feet, forcing Devendra to stop as well. "Vayu! Come on. You will grow fat if you eat any more. I want to see if there are people around." He had heard bards sing of the beauty of Mahendrapuri's Princess Hemangini. It was his curiosity that had brought him here today.

Hearing the sound of running feet, he turned around to see who it was. Even before he could realise what was happening, a slender form collided with his large and well-muscled frame. Letting go of Vayu's reins, Devendra lifted his hands to the young woman's shoulders, hoping to reduce the impact.

Princess Hemangini had been playing with her maids in the royal garden when she knocked against the stranger. She managed to sight him only when she was within a couple of feet. But by then, she couldn't stop her flying feet and the impact had been inevitable. Her heart galloped like a horse as she felt the muscular contours of a male form against her soft and luscious feminine body. At seventeen, the princess had never been within ten feet of any male, except for her father and her younger brother.

The hands holding her might have tried to be gentle, but they still felt as hard as iron. For one who had never been touched by a man, it felt as if she had been struck simultaneously by both thunder and lightning. Lifting her face up, her startled gaze met that of a complete stranger. Her eyelashes fluttering rapidly, she stared at his handsome face, wondering who he could be. She was tall, almost six feet. Even then, she had to look a long way up to see his face. When she caught him studying her face with equal curiosity and interest, soft colour rose up from her neck to her face, turning it pink.

Not one to feel shy of anyone, Hemangini continued to study his face boldly before asking, "Who are you? I have never seen you around this area before."

He smiled, the shapely lips below his thick moustache opening to reveal brilliant white teeth. "That is because I have never been here before today. And before I tell you who I am, who are you, beautiful lady?"

While the heat in her cheeks increased at the compliment, Hemangini felt her temper rising at his familiarity. "I am Princess Hemangini of Mahendrapuri!" she declared proudly, tilting her small chin up at him.

Devendra studied her beautiful face framed by thick, dark hair that had been gathered at her back. Her eyes were incredible, a strange shade of blue and violet framed by long and curling lashes, flashing every time she looked up at him. Her soft cheeks had turned pink in the evening sunlight, only adding to her lovely looks. As for her nose, with its *nathni*—her left nostril pierced to accommodate the golden ring— was slim and sharp. Right now, it was lifted up in the air in defiance. The dangling earrings that graced her ears were of rubies and diamonds set in gold as was the necklace she wore on her slender neck.

"I am happy to make your acquaintance, Your Highness!" he said, bowing his head to her, his hands still gripping her quivering shoulders. The bards had all been wrong. None of them could describe the princess's beauty, not by half. She was simply incredible, her soft lips naturally pink through which peeped small white teeth that gleamed like pearls. As for her figure—he quickly ran his gaze from her shoulders to her feet and up again before meeting her beautiful eyes—all he could think was that he had never come across anyone who was so perfectly shaped. Her shoulders were narrow while the breasts that rose and fell with each breath she took, appeared a handful. Oh yes! Big enough to fill his large hands. Her waist was small while the hips below were wide. Her legs were long while her feet were narrow. All in all, she was perfect, the top of her head just about reaching his shoulder.

She gave a regal nod before saying, "You still have not told me who you are."

He smiled again, wider than before, enhancing the grooves at the sides of his mouth, drawing her gaze to the dimples forming on his lean cheeks. "My name is Devendra."

Should the name mean something? Hemangini wasn't too sure. She suddenly realised that they were still standing too close to each other and her shoulders were even now trapped in his iron hard hands. She moved, trying to shrug off his hands only to find the hold becoming firmer than before. Her shoulders quivered as she lifted her hands to place them on his chest, doing her best to push him away. But it felt as if she was trying to move a mountain. What was worse was that she could feel the tremors in her hands due to the impact against his hard and muscular body. Removing them swiftly, she commanded, "Let me go." Would he? She wished she hadn't run so far away from her maids. None of them seemed to be within hearing distance. What if Devendra harmed her in some way? She looked up at him bravely, though with a wary look in her face.

With great reluctance, Devendra removed his hands from her shoulders, taking a couple of steps back. Even through her silk *uttariya*—the long scarf she wore across her breasts which fell over her shoulders—he couldn't help but feel the silkiness of her slender shoulders.

"Where are you from?" she asked, breathing easy. But deep down, a part of her was aware that she missed the warmth of his touch, even the hardness of it. Her shoulders tingled as blood flowed freely in the area that had grown almost numb as he had held her in his iron hard grip.

"I come from Indrapuri." He turned to his left to check if Vayu hadn't bolted away, before returning his gaze to her face.

"Are you a messenger?" she asked.

"Not really. I came hunting in the forest not far from here before I realised that I was pretty close to your kingdom. I thought it was time I met the royal family from our neighbouring kingdom."

Princess Hemangini stared at him, from the top of his turban with the beautiful *sarpech*, down to his broad feet covered in leather. The garments—a full-sleeved tunic and breeches—he wore, though made of simple cotton, were richly embroidered in gold thread. *Devendra! Have I heard the name before?*

He wore a long sword sheathed in a scabbard that hung from the leather belt at his waist and there was a quiver which was half full of arrows behind his left shoulder. The right shoulder sported an intricately carved bow. While he could have passed off for an ordinary warrior, she somehow felt there was more to him than met the eye.

"Come along with me," she said, turning away from him to walk in the opposite direction.

Quickly gathering Vayu's reins in his hand, Devendra followed her, his gaze avidly running over her long plaits that appeared to caress her firm buttocks as she delicately walked over the grass. He couldn't help noticing the firmly tied knot of her bustier in the middle of her otherwise bare back, her silk *uttariya* barely covering her shoulders.

They stopped at the stable on their way, Hemangini instructing the man in charge to take good care of their guest's horse. She noticed from the corner of her eyes that Devendra was reluctant to leave his horse with strangers. She couldn't really blame him considering that his Vayu was a highbred horse that was completely loyal to its owner. That was definitely a point in the man's favour, the consideration he had for a mere animal.

As for Devendra, he realised that he was deeply enamoured by the Princess of Mahendrapuri. But what about her? Could she be as attracted to him? He had to somehow garner her interest; for which he needed time. Towards that end, he had to make sure he was invited to be a guest of the royal family. His mind revolving around the different methods by which he could get his whim fulfilled, Devendra followed her as if in a trance.

The Princess of Mahendrapuri

The princess led Devendra to the main palace where her father, King Brahmabatra, resided. She was still struggling for composure when they reached the open doorway to the main hall, her body tingling from the impact of colliding hard against the stranger's muscular frame. The unfamiliar sensations had blurred her usually sharp brain. Even now, she was totally conscious of the tall and handsome man walking at her side. He obviously considered himself her equal or he would have walked a few steps behind, wouldn't he? Hemangini was curious to know who he was, the man who had such a regal air about him.

Entering the long hall where the king usually held court in the mornings, she walked further and turned left towards an entrance which was guarded by two sentries. They bowed when they saw that it was Princess Hemangini.

"Devendra, you may leave your weapons with the sentry here," she instructed the stranger before addressing one of the sentries, "Mahira! You must take care of them with your life and keep them safe."

The man gave a vigorous nod, saying, "I will do that, Your Highness!"

Devendra handed over his bow, arrows and sword to Mahira, touching his waistband to ensure that the knife he had tucked in there was safe. There was no way he was parting with that one, especially not when he was walking into a stranger's palace.

Stepping into the king's chamber with her head held high, Hemangini noticed that her father was not alone.

"*Pitashri!*" She walked forward swiftly and stood in front of the king, bowing her head even as she brought her hands together in a respectful greeting. "*Pranam!*"

"Hema, my dear child!" King Brahmabatra greeted her with a wide smile on his face, always happy to see his daughter. "What brings you here at this time of the evening? I was under the impression you were out in the garden playing with your friends."

"That is true, Father. I was playing outside when this stranger came by. This is Devendra from Indrapuri." She beckoned Devendra to step forward. "He wants to meet the royal family of Mahendrapuri is what he tells me."

"Devendra from Indrapuri!" The king immediately got up from his intricately carved and heavily cushioned throne, holding both his hands forward in greeting. "You must be the crown prince!" he declared, eyeing the younger man with wonder. "I wish you had sent word, Prince Devendra. We would have welcomed you with pomp. Welcome to the royal house of Mahendrapuri. I have heard so much about you and I am very happy to finally meet you in person." He took Prince Devendra's hands in his own and drew him to a chair adjacent to his. Clapping his hands, the king ordered the servant who walked into the chamber to bring some *madira* for their royal guest.

"Your Majesty Raja Brahmabatra! I am so happy to meet you as well. The bards sing highly of you and your kingdom."

Hemangini looked from their guest to her father and back to their guest again, unable to believe her ears. Could he really be the Prince of Indrapuri? Why hadn't he told her so when she asked him who he was? Sparks flew from her beautiful gaze when he turned to look at her, promising retribution for keeping her in the dark. She was unaware that the Prince of Indrapuri was completely enamoured by her and the tempestuous expression on her face only made him all the more enthralled.

The king introduced his chief minister and treasurer to Devendra before the two of them got up to take their leave. "You must stay with us, Prince Devendra. It would truly be an honour," invited King Brahmabatra, a warm smile on his face, completely unaware of the temper sparkling in his daughter's gaze.

Devendra was only too pleased that his wish had been granted without any effort on his part. Here was his opportunity to stay in the palace and get to know the princess well. Only too conscious of the princess's anger towards him, though he wasn't sure about the cause for it, Devendra gave his nod. "Thank you, Raja. I would be happy to spend some time here. I have heard a lot about your naval crafts and fishing activities."

"Oh yes!" Brahmabatra rubbed a hand over his salt and pepper beard as he looked at the prince. "I will personally take you to visit the seashore, Prince Devendra."

They conversed comfortably with each other as if they were old acquaintances while Princess Hemangini, who had also taken a seat by now, looked from one to the other, not participating in the same. She was extremely knowledgeable about Mahendrapuri's navy as well as the variety of fish it was renowned for. She was used to accompanying her father on most days when he rode to the seashore, from the time she was a child. Recently, with King Brahmabatra getting more and more involved in the court activities, she had taken to going there to supervise everything on his behalf.

Just now, she boldly studied Prince Devendra's face. That he was too handsome for words was the undeniable truth. The bards who visited their kingdom had all been in praise of the Prince of Indrapuri. She knew that he was some twenty-two summers old and the only child of Queen Kanchana Devi. She grimaced when she recalled the rumours she had heard, of King Chandrabhan maintaining a harem for his pleasure.

Hemangini bent her head slightly to hide her grimace. She simply couldn't tolerate the idea of her husband mating with other women. What a horrible idea! Though it was rather common, especially in royal households. Some kings even married more than one wife. Maybe the idea was to ensure that the lineage never ran out, but still, she didn't care for it, not at all. In that way, she truly admired her father. She had been her parents' only child until her brother Jaivardhan was born eight years later. But her parents had never been bothered about not having a son. And was Hemangini glad that her father had not considered getting another wife just because her mother, Queen Deepakala, had not given him a son!

The queen walked into the chamber just then. "Dinner has been served, Brahma. Why don't you...?"

It was only then that she noticed there was a third person, a stranger, sitting next to the king.

"Deepa, come and see who has decided to honour us with his visit today. Meet Rajkumar Devendra of Indrapuri. Devendra, this is my Rani, Deepamala."

"*Pranam*, Your Majesty!" Devendra got up from his chair to stand tall before the queen, greeting her with both hands folded.

That the queen was impressed by the neighbouring prince was putting it mildly. She looked into his handsome face and was taken up with his peaceful demeanour. "Welcome to our home, Rajkumar Devendra," she said, giving him a soft smile. The mother in her felt that he would make a perfect husband for her daughter. They had all heard so much about the prince's valour in battle; his compassion towards the citizens of Indrapuri and his intelligence while dealing with both friends and enemies. And wasn't it a good thing that Prince Devendra's kingdom wasn't too far away? They even had a common boundary.

"Thank you, Your Majesty. I am honoured to make your acquaintance."

"Shall we go to dinner?" King Brahmabatra got up from his seat to extend a hand towards the door leading to the dining hall.

"Definitely. I am ravenously hungry," said the prince, giving the royal couple a charming smile. When he noticed the princess from the corner of his eyes, he was startled to see her pout. Seeing her luscious lips gathered together, making them eminently kissable, he felt his body tighten in response.

Maybe he would have time to explore his feelings during the next few days while he spent time at Mahendrapuri. *I must send a message to my mother first thing in the morning,* he decided as he sat down to a sumptuous meal consisting of seven courses of well spiced exotic fish, meat, vegetables, and curries along with fluffy rice and barley grains. There were dates soaked in honey for dessert while *madira*—a high quality wine—was served along with each course.

"My compliments to your chef!" While Prince Devendra addressed the king as he lifted his silver cup to take a sip of wine from it, he eyed Princess Hemangini from where she was seated opposite him. He had noticed the delicate way she nibbled at her food, though she managed to eat good portions of each course. And she participated in the conversation going around as they all sat on the floor, crossing their legs in front of flat and beautifully carved wooden stools that held golden plates and bowls on which the food was served. Could the presence of her mother have loosened the princess's tongue?

His heart thudded heavily in his chest as he ran his gaze over her beautiful face and delicious body, wondering if he would get an opportunity to meet her alone, though it wouldn't be due to lack of trying on his part.

It was another hour before a manservant went along with the prince to show him to a guest chamber in another section of the king's palace. Overlooking the royal gardens at the back, the suite consisted of a sitting room, a bedroom and a veranda beyond it. The windows were all long and wide, circulating air into the rooms. There was a set of fresh robes laid on the bed which was covered with silk sheets.

"Please ring the bell if you need anything else, My Lord!" said the servant, pointing his hand to a small brass bell that was set on a carved wooden table beside the bed, bowing respectfully in front of the neighbouring kingdom's prince.

"I am sure I have everything I need," said the Prince, eyeing the silver jug of water on the bedstand along with an upturned silver tumbler, the utensils gleaming in the light of the brass lamps placed at strategic points all around the room. There was even a fire torch fitted on a bracket against one wall. "What's your name?"

"Dhoomaketu, My Lord!" The man responded, a look of surprise on his face. None of the royal guests who visited the Mahendrapuri palace—and there were many—had ever asked for his name or even spoken to him.

"Dhoomaketu! Why don't you wake me up in the morning just before sunrise? If I fail to wake up, that is." Devendra lifted an enquiring brow at the manservant.

"I will do that, My Lord!" He bowed himself out of the chamber, thrilled beyond measure that the prince had addressed him by his given name.

The bed was extremely comfortable and Devendra went to sleep the moment his head touched the pillow, enjoying a dreamless sleep.

A Sleepless Night

P rincess Hemangini was preoccupied with thoughts of the stranger—the one she now knew as Prince Devendra of Indrapuri—when she left the dining hall, wishing both her parents goodnight before stepping out. Her chief maids-in-waiting, Kalpana and Kamini, accompanied the princess to her suite of rooms which was a part of the queen's palace that was situated about five hundred feet away from the main palace.

As they walked across the garden, both the maids bombarded Hemangini with questions about the handsome stranger.

"I don't plan to tell you both anything," said the princess, her face portraying mock anger. "Where did you both disappear to when he arrived? I was waiting for you to come and rescue me."

"But, My Lady, we didn't think you needed rescuing, not from such a handsome prince." Kalpana teased her mistress, a grin on her gamine face.

"I don't see a reason to laugh," said the princess, turning her face to the other side to hide her own smile. "You cowards!" she insisted, returning her gaze to her friends once her expression was serious enough. "You have betrayed me, both of you."

Kamini, ever the pacifier, spoke quickly to ease the situation. "But you must admit that Prince Devendra is extremely handsome. How was it when you fell against his tall and muscular body? Did you feel something? Come on, you can tell us, My Lady. I am sure even Kalpana is dying to know." She winked at Princess Hemangini. Growing up together from childhood, the maids were more friends with the princess than her servants and behaved accordingly, with familiarity.

"Oh yes. Tell, tell, My Lady, please." Kalpana added her pleas to Kamini's, a wide grin on her face, her dark eyes crinkling at the corners with amusement.

Hemangini was glad that the crescent moon and twinkling stars weren't bright enough to betray the colour and heat which bloomed in her cheeks. She found the Prince of Indrapuri extremely charismatic. But that didn't mean she was going to admit it to anyone, not even to her close friends. The feeling was too new, too raw; so much so that she still hadn't had the opportunity to understand or come to terms with it.

She pouted at her friends, refusing to say anything as they walked on towards the princess's quarters. "My Lady…"

"Shh, Kamini. Let's talk tomorrow. I am too tired now." Hemangini cut off Kamini mid-sentence as they entered her chambers. "You may both leave. I want to sleep."

"But, My Lady! You will need help with your clothes and jewellery. Let me…" Kalpana's protest was cut short.

Hemangini wasn't keen to hear their chatter, her thoughts fluttering around Devendra. Whenever she thought of him—and it looked like it was every moment from the time she unexpectedly fell against his rock-hard chest—her heart felt as if it would burst out of her chest. That's how rapidly it beat against her ribcage. She wanted to be alone to truly understand what was happening to her. "Send Amala to me," she ordered before stepping into the main hall of her suite, her tone dismissive. Amala was mute and right now Hemangini would give anything for some peace and quiet which definitely wasn't available from within herself.

Kalpana and Kamini left, their steps reluctant. But they recognised an order when they heard one. Whispering between themselves, they quickly went to the maids' quarters which weren't too far away and beckoned to Amala. "The princess wants you to help her undress."

Amala gave an enthusiastic nod, a smile on her face as she almost ran to her mistress's rooms. She stepped inside and shut the doors to the chamber before walking further along through another door into the princess's bedroom. She brought her palms together in greeting and gave the princess a brilliant smile when the latter looked up from where she was seated on a velvet cushioned stool in front of the wide floor length mirror, fitted into a frame of teakwood, beautifully carved with animals and birds frolicking amongst a variety of flowers and plants.

"Come along and help me, Amala," invited the princess with a gentle smile on her face.

Amala quickly removed the strands of jasmine that were pinned to Princess Hemangini's hair before unravelling the three thick plaits that almost touched the carpeted floor now that the princess was seated.

She detached the golden hook that held the *maang tikka* from where it lay along the centre parting of the princess's hair with the pendant of diamonds and rubies covering the upper half of her forehead. Gently removing the piece of jewellery without hurting the princess, the maid placed it in a wooden box that lay open on the table in front of the mirror. Taking a wide-toothed comb delicately carved from ivory, she combed out the strands of hair before looping them in a loose knot at Hemangini's nape.

She helped remove the heavy dangling earrings and the necklace, also of rubies and diamonds, before removing the gold chain and twin-strands of milky pearls. Unhooking the *kamarbandh* of intricately carved gold from Hemangini's slim waist, the maid placed all the jewellery in separate boxes. Off came the *kadas* on her forearms and the finger rings before Amala knelt at the princess's feet. Taking a small and narrow foot in her left hand, she unhooked the anklet that shimmered in the lamplight. Looking up at the princess with a smile, the maid brought her thumb and forefinger together in a gesture of appreciation before removing the anklet from the other foot.

Amala got up to her feet to firmly massage the princess's shoulders, making the latter groan in delight. "Perfect, Amala," she said, smiling at her maid through the mirror. The maid grinned at Hemangini's appreciative words and continued to press her arms. It was a while before she untied the knot of the bustier and long skirt, both made of raw silk and embroidered with tiny pearls. Walking to one of the intricately carved wooden almirahs, the maid fetched a long cotton robe to wrap it around the princess.

"That will be all, Amala. You may go now." Princess Hemangini dismissed the mute maid with a smile on her face. Her head bowed, Amala left the princess alone, closing the bedroom doors behind her.

A long sigh burst forth from Hemangini when she finally found herself alone, her thoughts immediately rushing back to Prince Devendra. Kalpana and Kamini had both been curious about how she had felt when Hemangini fell against the prince. She shut her eyes to concentrate on her feelings at that moment.

Her breath came in gasps when she recalled the way her soft curves had fitted against the hard planes of his masculine frame. Her breasts tingled even now, the tips turning hard as the pebbles she used to collect from the seashore as a child. Before she was aware of what she was doing, Hemangini lifted both her hands and cupped her breasts, rubbing her palms against the tight buds. Not that her small hands could manage to cover the twin mounds which were the size of ripe melons. Her eyes glazing over and her cheeks turning pink, she bit her luscious lower lip as she imagined the prince's hands on her.

The princess had never felt such strange sensations on meeting a man, not ever! She gazed at her reflection in the mirror and was startled to see the seductive expression on her own face, her lips a deep red with repeated biting. Removing the heavy knot of hair at her nape, she let it fall loose at her back before shrugging out of her robe and staring at her naked form. Drawing her hair to the front from both sides, she let it fall over her breasts which played hide and seek between the dark strands, the brush of hair over her nipples invoking an unfamiliar depth of desire within her.

What will he think if he looked at her just now? Will he want to make her his? Hemangini dug the big toe of her right foot into the carpet, hugging herself, her fascinated eyes on the blush pink tip of a creamy breast peeping through all that hair.

The robe lay where she had dropped it over the dressing stool as she walked over to the bed. The princess's body felt too hot and the friction of the cotton robe was the last thing she wanted or needed against her person; not in the aroused state that she was in when she lay naked on the bed, running her hands over her form lazily; even as she imagined that the hands belonged to the prince. His iron hard touch on her shoulders had definitely left a powerful impression on the young princess's body and mind.

It was barely a short time before sunrise when sleep finally claimed her.

4

The Disappointed Prince

evendra was extremely disappointed when the beautiful Princess Hemangini didn't appear at breakfast. He didn't speak much as he partook of the meal along with the king, queen and Prince Jaivardhan.

The young prince of nine summers was talkative, taking away the onus of making conversation from Devendra. He chattered like a magpie, asking hundreds of questions about something or the other. His parents, the Raja and Rani of Mahendrapuri, answered him patiently, even as they made sure that Devendra was served a sumptuous meal.

Devendra didn't notice the queen eyeing him from time to time as he stared broodingly at his plate wondering where the princess was. If Hemangini didn't turn up soon, he had a good mind to go in search of her. He sincerely hoped that King Brahmabatra would be too busy at court, and only too relieved if Devendra offered to explore the surroundings by himself. But before that, he had to get away from the king without coming across as rude.

Once breakfast was over, Devendra wiped his hands and mouth on a cotton napkin before addressing King Brahmabatra. "Your Majesty! I am sure you are going to be busy at court. I am thinking of taking a ride around your kingdom if that is alright with you."

Brahmabatra gave his royal guest a relieved smile. He had been wondering himself how he was going to entertain the visiting prince amidst his busy schedule. After all, the prince's stay at Mahendrapuri was unplanned. "If you are sure, Prince Devendra. I could send someone along with you as escort."

Devendra nodded. "Will you be able to spare Mahira?" He had liked the young and enthusiastic sentry he had met the earlier evening outside the king's door.

"I am sure that can be arranged, Rajkumar."

"I will also need a messenger to take a note to my mother," said Devendra, getting to his feet. He had already scratched out a quick note to his mother on a palm leaf scroll, rolled it into a silver holder and sealed it before tucking it into his waistband.

The king waved a hand at one of the assistants surrounding them, indicating that the matter should be taken care of. "If you will give me leave, Prince Devendra? I will meet you for lunch."

"Thank you, Your Majesty!" Once the king left the dining hall, Devendra handed over the silver holder to one of Brahmabatra's assistants who came forward to receive it. "This needs to be personally handed over to my mother, Rani Kanchana Devi, at the Indrapuri palace."

"Sure, My Lord! It will be taken care of," said the man, bowing low before the prince.

"Tell your man to wait for a reply and bring it along with him," said the prince in a voice of authority before turning to Queen Deepamala and her son. "If I may take your leave, Your Highness and Prince Jaivardhan?"

The queen smiled, giving him a nod even as Jaivardhan giggled, waving to their guest. Only after

Devendra walked out of the dining room did Queen Deepamala allow a frown to crease her forehead. She was too irritated with her daughter. This wasn't the right time to sleep late, not when a highly eligible prince was staying with them. She waited for someone to escort young Prince Jaivardhan to his classroom before walking over to the other palace, with a good mind to give her daughter a thorough scolding.

"Mother!" Hemangini turned a glowing face to Deepamala when the queen entered the main hall of the princess's chamber. Dressed in an emerald green silk *antariya* that fell down to her ankles with a matching bustier and *uttariya* carelessly draped over her left shoulder, all embroidered with shimmering gold thread and diamonds, the young lady sparkled in the sunlight streaming through the open windows. The *antariya* was draped in folds down the length of her long legs, giving her the freedom to sit astride a horse. It was held together at the waist by a *kamarbandh* of beaten gold embellished with diamonds and emeralds, as were the rest of her jewellery right from the top of her sleek head to her dainty ankles. Turning round in a pirouette, the princess asked her mother, "How do I look?"

Queen Deepamala pouted at her daughter before gesturing for her maids to leave them alone. "Are you going riding?" she asked, without replying to Hemangini's question.

"Mother! You haven't answered me," grumbled Hemangini, eyeing her mother through the mirror once the others left.

Deepamala smiled at her beautiful child. "You look lovely, Hema, as you well know it. But that doesn't stop me from being angry with you." She gave the princess a mock glare, her heart too full of love for her firstborn to be really angry with her.

"But why, Mother?" Hemangini turned to her mother to give her a hug, kissing her on her cheek.

"Why didn't you come for breakfast? I am sure the Rajkumar of Indrapuri missed you."

"And how would you know? Did he tell you so?" asked Hemangini, a hand at her chest as if to calm down her heart that beat like a jungle drum even as colour rushed up her cheeks.

Studying her daughter's blushing face, the queen smiled. "Not everything needs to be put into words, you know. The prince didn't have to say anything. But I could see his searching gaze every time someone walked into the dining hall. But wait! That's not the point. Why didn't you come?" She was relentless in her questioning. The queen was eager to have her daughter tie the knot with the neighbouring kingdom's prince. Indrapuri was a powerful kingdom and it would make great political sense to get together with the royal family. What better way to have the crown prince of the kingdom wed the Princess of Mahendrapuri? That Prince Devendra was handsome, intelligent and courageous only made the idea more and more attractive.

While she was enamoured with the idea of Princess Hemangini wedding Prince Devendra, Queen Deepamala would never force her daughter to choose a man she didn't care for. But looking at the young lady's blushing face on hearing the prince's name, the queen realised that her daughter was definitely aware of the neighbouring prince, if not more.

Hemangini's mouth drooped at the corners. *As if I don't want to spend time with Devendra!* It was her turn to pout at her mother. "I was awake till late in the night, Mother. And the sun was up when Kalpana could finally wake me up."

No way was she going to share that scene with her mother. She had been lying naked on her bed when the maid had walked in before sunrise, so deeply asleep that no amount of shaking could bring her awake. After all, she had been awake until the time when the sun's rays were already turning the eastern sky pink. Unable to wake her mistress up, Kalpana had finally given up after covering Hemangini with a silken sheet.

Both Kalpana and Kamini had teased the princess mercilessly when she finally woke up much later. Hemangini had missed her long and luxurious bath in the private pool enclosed by myriad trees which was part of her daily morning routine, and had had to make do with a quick wash in an enclosed bathing room.

Queen Deepamala looked her daughter up and down, curious about her daughter's sleepless night. Could it be because Hemangini was conscious of the visiting prince as an attractive man? Rubbing her hands together in glee, she said, "After breakfast, the Prince mentioned that he was going for a ride along with Mahira. Maybe you...?"

Quickly walking to the entrance of her chamber and slipping her small feet into moulded leather slippers, Hemangini rushed out of her suite. "I will see you later, Mother."

"What about breakfast...?" The princess was gone before Deepamala completed her sentence. A broad smile lit up the queen's face as she stared in the direction her daughter had taken, pleased to note that it was towards the royal stables.

Hemangini's plan was to have the stable master saddle Agni, her brilliant white horse. She was going to find Prince Devendra even if she had to scout the whole kingdom.

She came to a halt suddenly, her face turning a fiery red as she teetered on her feet when she noticed Devendra walking out of the stable with Vayu's reins in his hand. He looked even more handsome this morning, the sun's rays caressing his lean face. His cheeks were gleaming, obviously having been freshly shaved that morning, his moustache thick and curled up on both sides of his face. His deep eyes were a dark brown, crinkling at the corners. He had done away with his turban, his head bare, the dark and curly hair falling down to his broad and heavily-muscled shoulders.

"Good morning to you, Rajkumari Hemangini," he greeted her in a gruff voice. What a sight she made in her emerald green attire! Her hair was rolled up in a complicated knot at the back of her head while her tiny waist appeared smaller than ever with the gold *kamarbandh* studded with precious stones. As for her face, it glowed in the sunlight, the luscious lips invitingly damp, making him crave for her kisses. The large earrings and necklace only added to her beauty.

"Good morning, Rajkumar Devendra!" She took a deep breath before replying to his greeting, giving him a small nod. No way was she going to let him know that her heart was beating so hard that it was on the verge of suffocating her.

"I missed you at breakfast." There! The words were out before he could stop them.

Heat invaded her cheeks as she eyed him with her shining lavender gaze. "Did you now? I slept late."

He tilted his head in acknowledgement. "I was planning to go for a ride. Would you like to join me?"

Wouldn't she! The exact reason why she had raced to the stables just now. "I would like that. Give me a moment and I'll have my horse saddled."

The stable master stepped out with the saddled Agni. "Greetings, Rajkumari Hemangini! Agni is all ready to go. I saddled him when I heard your voice outside."

Hemangini gave the man a grateful smile, taking hold of the reins as she prepared to climb on Agni's back. But before she could put her foot in the stirrup, she was startled to find herself being lifted by two strong hands and placed on the back of her horse. Her whole body quivered at the touch of Devendra's hands on her bare waist. He seemed to require no effort for lifting her completely off her feet.

Planning to blast him off, she turned her head to glare at him only to melt like butter when she met his fiery gaze that reminded her of molten honey. Her eyelashes fluttered rapidly against her cheeks and the princess bent her head to pat her horse with a trembling hand, her breath coming in gasps. The touch of those iron hard hands on her shoulders yesterday had kept her awake for most of last night. And now he had given her one more memory of the same hands on her slender and bare waist. It felt as if she had been branded by those masculine hands. As thoughts flashed in her mind of where all his hands could wander over her body, the princess touched her whip to Agni's flank. The horse responded with alacrity, taking off like the wind itself, Prince Devendra thundering right behind on Vayu.

5

The Messenger from Mahendrapuri

ryavaan, the messenger from Mahendrapuri, reached Indrapuri two days later, carrying Devendra's message safely tucked in his waistband. Reaching the gates to the royal palace, he jumped off his horse before speaking to the guard, requesting him for an audience with Queen Kanchana Devi.

"Where are you from? And what is the purpose of your meeting with our queen?" asked Sarnath, the sentry at the gates.

"I am from Mahendrapuri and have come here on Rajkumar Devendra's orders," said Aryavaan, puffing up his chest in importance.

Sarnath frowned at the man who was holding the reins of his horse. The horse was dusty and the man's clothes were wrinkled, as if the two had travelled a long way. Not caring that the man appeared tired, the sentry asked the visitor in a voice tinged with mockery, "Is Mahendrapuri's prince also called Devendra?" As far as Sarnath knew, the other kingdom's prince was a mere child and his name was definitely not Devendra.

Are all the citizens of Indrapuri stupid or is it just this guard? Aryavaan frowned as he thought to himself. "My man, doesn't your Indrapuri have a prince named Devendra?" he asked, his voice highly sarcastic.

"Don't you dare take our prince's name in vain. Or I will have your tongue pulled out." Sarnath's huge body bristled with temper as he glared at the visitor, raising his hands to rub them against his thick and well-oiled moustache, twisting them at the ends in a challenging gesture.

"Look here! I have an important message to deliver to your Rani Kanchana Devi. If you are not going to allow me to do my duty, then let it be on your head. I am going right back to Mahendrapuri and will tell Rajkumar Devendra about the fools who work as sentries in his kingdom." Aryavaan turned around, a foot already in the stirrup as he pretended to leave.

"*Arre re*! Stop! Stop! Calm down, my man." Sarnath rushed forward, his bulky body swinging from side to side before he reached across to place a hand on the visitor's arm. "Get off your horse, man. Now I understand that you have a message from our Rajkumar Devendra which is to be delivered to our Rani Kanchana Devi. Why didn't you make yourself clear first itself?"

Aryavaan gave the guard a scornful look before removing his foot from the stirrup and placing it on the ground. "Take me to your Rani immediately."

Sarnath shook his head. "No, no, that's not possible. You will first need to go to the travellers' choultry and book yourself a room. Then have a bath and meal. There will be people to care of your horse as well. Once you are neatly turned out, you may seek audience with the Rani." How he enjoyed making people feel uncomfortable! Especially those who were new to his kingdom and its customs.

Aryavaan sighed. He had been sure that his mission was a matter of urgency and he would get to meet the Queen of Indrapuri immediately. But it didn't seem so. Looking the gigantic guard up and down, he asked, "How do I get to this travellers' choultry?"

"You go straight for some time before you reach a circle with the statue of our king's grandfather, Maharaja Suryabhan, sitting on a horse." He continued when the visitor nodded, "From there you take a right. Soon, you will see the temple tower of Lord Shiva. You cannot miss it as it stands tall against the skies." There was immense pride in his voice when he uttered the fact. "The choultry is right at the back of this temple."

Aryavaan gave the guard a nod before going on his way. It looked like he might have to stay the night in Indrapuri, not exactly what he had planned. But then, he mentally shrugged to himself, he could not leave the kingdom until he had completed his duty for which he had travelled all the way—to personally handover the Indrapuri's prince's message to his queen mother. Patting his waistband to check that the silver message holder was in place, he rode through the capital city, looking to the left and to the right, fascinated by not just the fruit trees and flowering plants, but even the people who were clothed differently from his own. Soon, he reached the marketplace before a smile widened his mouth. The sounds of the busy area were very similar to Mahendrapuri and made him feel at home. Humming to himself, he continued to ride at a steady pace.

It was evening before Aryavaan found himself in the presence of the Queen of Indrapuri. Bowing low to the level of his waist, he said, "*Pranam*, Your Majesty! I am Aryavaan from Mahendrapuri. I have been sent here by Rajkumar Devendra who is a guest at our Raja Brahmabatra's palace. The Rajkumar of Indrapuri sent me here to deliver a message to you personally, Your Majesty." He removed the silver holder and handed it to a deputy minister who was also present in the hall of the queen's chambers.

The deputy minister broke the seal at the queen's nod, removing the palm leaf scroll and handing it to Kanchana Devi respectfully.

Unrolling the scroll, the queen read the message from her son quickly, a beautiful smile stretching across her face and softening it. Her son Devendra was to be a guest in King Brahmabatra's palace for a few weeks. In the meanwhile, he had plans to woo the Princess of Mahendrapuri. He had also mentioned that his mother should probably make arrangements for a royal wedding to be announced in the not-too-far future. Queen Kanchana Devi was extremely happy that her son had finally found a princess he wanted to wed. She had been getting worried about her husband's second born, Prince Gagandeep— Queen Paromita's elder son — getting married before her own son. *What if Gagandeep fathered a son before Devendra and that child was declared the heir to the throne?* She shuddered at the thought which terrorised her, keeping her awake on many nights.

Thrilled at the prospect of organising her son's marriage soon, she took a handful of gold coins from the silver tray lying next to her chair and dropped them in the messenger's hands. "You have brought me good news, Aryavaan." Turning to the deputy minister, she said, "Make sure that he has a comfortable stay before he returns to Mahendrapuri."

The deputy minister nodded. "I will do that, Your Majesty." Turning to the messenger, he said, "Come with me, my man."

Aryavaan didn't move. Bowing to the queen again, he said, "Rajkumar Devendra was insistent that I take him back your reply, Your Majesty."

The queen smiled. "You will have it before you leave tomorrow. Go with the minister now," she dismissed the messenger from Mahendrapuri.

Aryavaan went along with the minister, excited about the coins tucked in his waistband. There were five of them, all gold, that the queen had given him. It was a lot of riches and will suffice to run his household for a whole year. Was he glad that he had been the chosen one to bring Prince Devendra's message down to his mother!

A Secret Plan

I t had been five days since Devendra came to stay at the Mahendrapuri palace. He found himself more and more enamoured by the lovely Princess of Mahendrapuri. She was not just a beautiful face, but an intelligent conversationalist as well. She was educated and was also trained in sword fighting and archery. As for her horse-riding skills, the prince was only too impressed with them as she took him riding around her kingdom. The royal palaces were in the centre, around which were built the grand homes for the ministers. The third circle was of houses for the common citizens interspersed by markets situated in four pockets. The final circle was for the buildings that housed the warriors and their families. This was also divided into four arcs, with each corner allotted for a specific purpose. Stables were built for the war horses in one corner while the second corner housed the war elephants. The third corner was where the weaponry was situated, ironsmiths forging swords, arrows, spears and more through the day, the clang of metal against metal resounding in the area. The fourth corner was allotted for military training.

Devendra could see that the kingdom was well planned and the people were extremely happy with their lot. Brahmabatra was obviously a kind and just ruler, his citizens loyal to him.

"The naval base is beyond this wall," said Hemangini, pointing at the fortress wall to her right. "We have a fleet of twenty ships, each one capable of carrying two hundred warriors," she explained, her eyes shining with pride.

Devendra nodded, giving her a smile. "Do you get many enemies across the waters?" he asked.

She shook her head. "None during my lifetime. Though I have heard father speaking about enemies from some islands down south called Lakshadweepam. They attacked Mahendrapuri when my grandfather was king."

"I have heard about the warriors of Lakshadweepam. They are ferocious and don't follow any rules." Devendra gave her an awed look, wondering who had won that particular battle.

Hemangini laughed, the sound like the tinkling of silver bells, bringing an answering smile to his face. "That's right. They were unlawful, but no match for my grandfather and his navy. I don't have to tell you that we won."

"I am so glad to hear that," he said, running his gaze from the top of her bejewelled head to the tips of her toes peeping out of the leather sandals strapped to her narrow feet. The brilliant red of her clothes today made her glow all the more in the sunlight. Every day, they had been accompanied by two of her men. How he wished he could get her alone to himself!

The princess turned her head to look at the prince when she felt his gaze studying her. How was it even possible that he grew handsomer day by day?! Sleep continued to elude her at nights though she never made the mistake of waking up late after the first morning. She spent all her waking hours in his company. It looked as if her parents were really keen that she got to know their guest better.

While she liked the idea, what truly frustrated Hemangini was that they were always surrounded by other people. If no one else, it was Mahira and Bahula who rode with them every day. She had warned her friends Kalpana and Kamini to stay away. Though they both didn't like it at all, they heeded the princess's words and stayed back at the palace day after day. It was only at night, just before Hemangini went to sleep, did the two of them pester her with questions.

"Has the Prince of Indrapuri fallen in love with you yet?" asked Kalpana, helping the princess change for the night.

Hemangini frowned at her maid through the mirror. "How would I know if the prince is in love with me or not? You had better ask him," she pouted. Right now, she would kill to know the answer to that particular question. As each day passed, she found herself more and more attracted to their royal guest. But he showed no signs of feeling anything special for her. He had not even tried to spend time alone with her. Her features tightened as quick anger rose from within. Was he interested in her at all? Why did he put up with her guards? Couldn't he take her away from them and spend some time alone, just the two of them? She gritted her teeth, her jaw aching with tension.

Kamini met Kalpana's eyes over the princess's head. Throughout the day, the maids had both been chatting about their princess and Prince Devendra from the neighbouring kingdom. Maybe it was time to help the prince and princess along, pushing them gently in the right direction. When Kalpana gave a nod, Kamini spoke, "My princess, why don't you invite him to spend time with you in the garden tomorrow afternoon?"

Temper flared in the lavender eyes that sparked fire at the maid's words. "Along with Mahira and Bahula? I am not interested," she said sharply.

Kalpana giggled. "The two of them will also come with the prince, of course."

"What is there to laugh about?" Hemangini snarled. "Why the garden of all places? What does it matter anyway?" She jumped up from the dressing stool and paced the room up and down.

"My Lady! Don't forget to invite the two of us as well," said Kamini, walking forward to stand in front of the princess, stopping her in her tracks.

"As if those two jokers are not enough, you want me to invite the two of you too…" She stopped talking when light dawned on her face, her mouth stretching into a wide smile. "You both will keep the guards busy and distracted."

"Exactly." Kalpana joined the two of them to laugh out loud. "Do you feel better now, My Lady?"

Hemangini threw her arms around her maids and hugged them close. "What will I do without the two of you!" Her heart beat hard with excitement as she thought of spending time with Devendra, just the two of them. She would take him to the arbour in the west corner which was the furthest area from the palace. Perfect!

7

The Queens' Minds
Think Alike

I t was late in the night when Queen Deepamala got around to having a chat with her husband. "Brahma, what do you think of Rajkumar Devendra?" she asked, folding the freshly plucked betel leaf around the many aromatic ingredients—crushed betelnuts, roasted fennel seeds, cardamom, clove, palm sugar and more—the palace chef had put together and handing it over to the king.

Holding the *paan* in his hand, the king lifted an enquiring brow at his wife. "You mark my words: Devendra will make a great king one day. He will be an even better ruler than his father, Raja Chandrabhan."

"Do you really think so?" asked Deepamala, her eyes going wide in awe. This was getting better and better. Somehow, she had to make sure that Devendra agreed to wed their daughter. Imagine Hemangini becoming the Queen of Indrapuri! The kingdom was at least four times the size of their own Mahendrapuri. With Hemangini married to the future King of Indrapuri, they would never have to worry about an attack from their neighbours for one thing. For another, enemies will think twice before attacking the *sambandhis* of the powerful ruler of Indrapuri. All in all, it would be so perfect! She looked at her husband eagerly, awaiting his response.

"I know so. Have you noticed the way the Prince of Indrapuri walks and talks? He treats everyone with such respect and compassion. And he hasn't gained those muscular shoulders and iron hard body by sitting back on his throne. The other day, when I visited the training ground, I saw Devendra in action. Believe me when I say that I was absolutely impressed with his sword wielding skills."

Queen Deepamala pouted at her husband who had finally managed to place the *paan* in his mouth and begun chewing on it. "I never get a chance to see such things. You never take me to the training ground, ever," she complained.

The king gave his queen a startled glance. It had never struck him that she might be interested in matters of the war. "I thought you didn't care for fights," he said, shifting the *paan* to one side of his mouth.

"Generally, no. But this was something special. And I am deviating from what I wanted to speak to you about. Brahma, what do you think of an alliance between the kingdom of Indrapuri and our Mahendrapuri?" she asked, watching Brahmabatra's face carefully. She had a reason for it. So far, on behalf of Princess Hemangini, her husband had rejected the hands of at least twenty-two princes from as many kingdoms. According to Brahmabatra, no prince was good enough for his darling daughter. He tended to find some fault or the other and rejected every alliance.

The king, who had been reaching out for his spittoon, lifted his head with a jerk at the queen's question, a surprised expression on his face. Spitting the remnants of the betel leaf in a hurry, he wiped his face with the end of his *uttariya* that was lying beside him before giving Deepamala his complete attention. "Are you talking about a wedding between Rajkumar

Devendra and our Hema?" he asked, a small frown pleating his forehead, drawing his thick eyebrows together.

Deepamala's lips drooped at the corners on perceiving his frown while she hoped against hope that her husband wouldn't reject the idea outright. "Please don't say no. Just think about it. Prince Devendra is the heir to Indrapuri's throne. You have already mentioned that he's a brave warrior. You must have noticed that he's well-mannered too. And just think about it, Brahma. Think of Hema and Devendra together! Don't you think they appear like Lord Mahavishnu and Goddess Mahalakshmi when they walk together?" The mother was keen to have her daughter married to the valiant prince.

"Hmm." The king placed a fist under his chin, considering his wife's words, a faraway look in his eyes as he continued to frown.

Deepamala kept her silence. Deep within, her heart rejoiced, all because of the reason that Brahmabatra hadn't rejected the proposal outright. That in itself seemed very encouraging to her.

It was a while before the frown disappeared from King Brahmabatra's face and he smiled at his wife. "I think you are right, Deepa. It's a really great idea to form an alliance with the Indrapuri kingdom. What better way than to marry Hema to their prince? It's a wonder that I never thought along those lines all this long. I am happy that you did though, my dear."

Queen Deepamala was thrilled beyond measure. Now that her husband was convinced, she was confident that he would leave no stone unturned to make sure that the alliance was brought about.

Queen Kanchana Devi had to wait two days after she received the message from her son Devendra before she could meet her husband King Chandrabhan in private. With so many queens taking up his attention, the King of Indrapuri visited her only on one night of the week. While it made her furious, she curbed her temper only because she needed to ask Chandrabhan for a favour.

"Chandra!"

"Kanchana, my dear." He sat on the bed next to her, a smile on his face. "You look happy."

"I am happy, now that you are here with me," she said, tilting her chin at him.

"As I am happy to be with you," he said, taking her hand in his.

"Is that the truth, My Lord?" She gave him a corner-eyed glance.

"You know very well that I never utter a lie. But tell me, where is Devendra nowadays? It has been a week since I set eyes on him."

"Which is what I have been meaning to talk to you about, My Lord. Devendra is visiting with the royal family of Mahendrapuri."

"Really! How did this come about so suddenly?" asked the king.

"Devendra went hunting some days ago in the Bhima Forest. When they reached the clearing on the other side, he realised that he was close to Mahendrapuri. That's when he decided to pay them a visit."

Chandrabhan sat up on the bed, getting up from his relaxed position. "You mean he simply went there without an invitation?" He frowned at his wife, not liking what he was hearing.

"Our son will never do that. He was curious to see the neighbouring kingdom and went there. I believe the king recognised him immediately and invited him with great respect to spend some time with them." Kanchana Devi bit the inside of her cheek, hoping that she had not said the wrong thing. If Chandrabhan decided to take offence, then there was no way he would agree to what she was going to suggest to him just now.

"Hmm. Devendra is not a child any more. He can't lose his respect by casually visiting other kingdoms," said Chandrabhan firmly.

"What you say is true, Chandra. But then, how will he get to know about the world if he stays within the borders of our kingdom all the time?" asked Kanchana Devi.

Chandrabhan stared at her for a few minutes before seeing the sense in her words. "I presume that your son has sent you a message?"

"*Our* son has sent a message, yes. And it's all good news." She gave him a wide smile, lifting a hand to place it on his shoulder. "You will be happy to know that Devendra is finally interested in marriage."

"Is he now?" The king lifted an eyebrow in query. "Is it just marriage in general or does he want to marry someone in particular?" Gaining an answer from the expression on her face, he continued, "It had better be a worthy princess, Kanchana. Otherwise, I will never agree," said the king firmly.

Kanchana Devi laughed softly, running her hand down the king's chest. "I know that you will not refuse this alliance. He is keen to wed Hemangini, the Princess of Mahendrapuri. You cannot deny that she's a princess worthy of our son and suitable to become the future Queen of Indrapuri." She gave him a triumphant glance.

He gave a slow nod, having no reason to disagree with her. If they could have an alliance with Mahendrapuri, their own kingdom would become that much stronger. And he had heard a lot about the beauty and grace of Princess Hemangini. It looked like Devendra had chosen well. "Why don't you talk to the astrologer and see if there is a suitable *muhurat* for the wedding?"

Kanchana Devi felt jubilant. Finally! Finally, she would be able to ensure that Devendra ascended the throne after her husband. "I will do that," she promised, burying her face in her husband's chest.

The Arbour Rendezvous

deep frown drew Devendra's dark eyebrows together when he saw the princess that morning. It looked like it hadn't been enough that two men had accompanied them every day till now. Today, two maids had come along with her. Will he ever get an opportunity to spend time alone with the Princess of Mahendrapuri? Controlling the huge sigh of frustration that threatened to escape his throat, he gave her a gentle smile when he greeted her, "Good morning, Rajkumari Hemangini."

"Good morning, Rajkumar Devendra." Hemangini felt her heart pick up speed when she noticed the frown of frustration on the prince's face. So! It looked like he was as irritated with other people surrounding the two of them, just as she was.

"Where are we going today?"

"I was wondering if you would like to go to the royal garden. We can walk. While maybe our horses could do with some rest," she said, grinning mischievously up at him, her beautiful eyes shining in the morning light.

Staring at her luscious lips and pearly teeth, he felt his body go hard with need. Just now, he would have walked all the way to hell if she was going to accompany him. "I would love to go to the garden with you," he said, his voice gruff. Did he dare take her hand in his? But then, why not? Quickly putting his thought to action, he reached for her hand and held it in his firm clasp.

Her heart jumped to her throat as she felt her hand being held in his iron hard hold. Did the prince not know the meaning of gentleness? But then again, her hand seemed to welcome that hard grip as it lay in his grasp. It was an effort to curb her instinct to lay her head on his broad shoulder as Hemangini walked at his side, her slender arm brushing against his muscled one. By now, both of them seemed to have forgotten all about the four people accompanying them.

Kalpana and Kamini played their roles to perfection as they chatted with Mahira and Bahula, making eyes at them and distracting them completely from the royal couple who walked ahead. It wasn't long before Hemangini drew Devendra into the arbour which gave them enough privacy what with tall trees at the back and climbers on both sides and above as they twisted around the metal frame which was set up for exactly such a purpose. The climbers with fragrant and colourful flowers were so thick that very little sunlight could penetrate through them. There was a seat of granite in the middle of the arbour.

Finally noticing that their escorts had been left behind, Devendra stopped frowning, sitting down on the seat before pulling Hemangini down next to him. He still hadn't let go of her hand as he turned sideways to look at her lovely face.

A sudden shyness gripped the princess when she realised that they were completely alone, just the two of them. Her head felt too heavy for her neck as she looked down at the grass, even as she dragged her big toe through the soil. Her heart beat so hard that she wondered if it might choke her. As for her hand, it still lay in the prince's hold which had tightened by now.

"Hemangini…"

She turned her startled gaze to his when she felt the whisper close against her ear, his breath teasing the tendrils of hair dancing in the soft breeze.

Her nervous gaze reminded him of a gazelle that was on the verge of fleeing. Releasing her hand, he lifted his own to place it on her slender shoulder.

"Sss…" Her cheeks resembled the colour of vermilion as colour gushed up her face at his touch; all because her *uttariya* had slipped off her right shoulder, leaving it bare. The warmth of his touch on her bare skin made her shiver with longing for she knew not what.

"Am I hurting you?" he asked in a gentle voice, thrilled to notice the colour on her cheeks. Not that he let go of her shoulder, his palm rejoicing in the texture of her silky skin. *Will her whole body feel as soft and silky as the slender shoulder?* He couldn't help wondering as he lowered his gaze to her luscious breasts that rose and fell heavily with every breath she took.

Hemangini shook her head, unable to look into his eyes again, only too aware of his heated gaze on her breasts. Her nipples turned hard as pebbles even as her breath came out in gasps. Had she made a mistake bringing the prince here to this private area? Now that they were alone, she wasn't so sure that she had made a wise decision.

"Hemangini, look at me." A hand at her chin, Prince Devendra lifted her face up to his.

While she couldn't stop her face being lifted up to his, Princess Hemangini felt her eyelids pressing down over her eyes, suddenly feeling too heavy to be raised even as an unfamiliar shyness gripped her in its thrall. Her dark and curly eyelashes fluttered on her cheeks as she made a great effort to lift her eyelids, which came to no avail.

Smiling, Devendra reached forward to press his mouth to her forehead, the brush of his moustache against her sensitised skin making her shudder with longing. "You look beautiful, my princess. It has been a long week waiting to meet you alone."

The heavy eyelids lifted suddenly as she gave him a fiery glance. "You never made an effort to meet me alone," she accused, her lips pouting attractively.

Laughter creased the corners of Prince Devendra's mouth as he grinned at her. "You forget that I am your father's guest. I cannot prey on my host's daughter."

"Is that so? Then what are you doing now?" she asked, tilting her chin challengingly up at him.

He shrugged his broad shoulders, drawing her gaze to them, totally oblivious to the effort she had to put in to hold up her dropping jaw. "The matter is out of my hands. If the Princess of Mahendrapuri has arranged to meet me in private, I, as a mere guest, can only oblige." He shook with laughter even as he caressed her blushing cheek with his thumb.

Intelligent and courageous! As much as he was handsome and well-mannered. Was it any surprise that he had stolen her heart! Lifting a small fist, she hit him on a muscular arm in response to his teasing. When he laughed some more, she buried her face in his chest, her face heating up even more as her heart galloped as fast as Agni when he raced through the plains. She sighed deeply when she felt his caressing hand at the back of her head.

Devendra wasn't laughing any more as he held her body close to his chest, relishing the contrast as her soft curves fitted into his hard planes. He had to make her his, soon. Tugging at her hair to pull her face up to his, he said, "I would like to make you my wife, princess. Will you be mine?"

Hemangini looked up into his dear face, struck with wonder at the need and desire in his gaze before responding, "I would be honoured, Prince Devendra."

"I am Deven to you, my princess," he whispered into her ear before pressing his lips to her soft cheek.

"You must call me Hema, my prince."

The Ardent Prince

By the next morning, Aryavaan, the messenger, had returned from Indrapuri, bringing with him the same silver holder which Prince Devendra had handed over to him to be delivered to his mother. Now, it held a palm leaf scroll with a message from Queen Kanchana Devi.

"My Lord!" Aryavaan bowed low before Devendra.

"Aryavaan! I hope you had a good trip to my kingdom." Devendra raised his hand in acknowledgement.

"Yes, My Lord! Your mother, Her Highness Rani Kanchana Devi, sent this for you," said the messenger, reaching into his waistband to remove the silver holder and offering it to the prince with great reverence.

"Excellent, my man. Here you go." The prince handed a gold mohur to the messenger.

Aryavaan bowed low as he thanked the Prince of Indrapuri before asking, "May I serve you in some other way, My Lord?"

"Thank you, Aryavaan. I will call for you if there is a need. You may go now." Devendra dismissed the messenger, more interested in breaking the seal on the silver holder that contained his mother's message.

Opening the scroll, he smiled when he read his mother's letter. She was thrilled about the fact that he was interested in marrying Princess Hemangini of Mahendrapuri. It wouldn't be long before she and his father, King Chandrabhan, would come over here to celebrate his wedding. She had even consulted the royal astrologer and fixed a date three weeks from now. His father had also sent a separate message to King Brahmabatra regarding the matter.

This was too good a revelation to keep to himself. He had to meet Hemangini and tell her about it. Getting up from where he was seated in the main hall of his chamber, Prince Devendra swiftly stepped out with the intention of asking someone for the princess's whereabouts, only to find her walking in the direction of the main palace, accompanied by her maids. Realising that she must be on her way to meet her father, he intercepted her. "Hema…"

Even though at least five feet separated them, his gruff tone sent a shiver down her spine as Princess Hemangini stopped in front of Prince Devendra. She had chosen to wear a silk skirt and bustier, the brilliant pink of the lotus bud that could be found in the ponds that were aplenty in the royal gardens; heavily embroidered in gold and tiny diamonds along with matching jewellery. Her hair was held up in an intricate knot at the back of her head. "Deven…" she responded, her voice a shy whisper, ignoring her giggling maids who stood far behind out of respect to their princess and the visiting prince. The time she had spent in his arms the earlier day had been heavenly. But it had been nowhere near enough nor had it dissolved her shyness completely.

"The messenger I sent to my kingdom has returned. He has not only brought a letter for me from my mother, but another one from my father to Raja Brahmabatra as well." He studied her face eagerly, keen that she understood the importance of what he was saying.

Her mouth open, she stared at him wide-eyed. "What do you think Raja Chandrabhan must have written to my father about? Not about us..." Her eyelashes fluttered on her cheeks like butterfly wings even as colour flooded her face.

Devendra grinned. "You are intelligent, my princess. And you are absolutely right. My mother has already met with the royal astrologer of Indrapuri and has fixed a date for our wedding in three weeks' time."

Her heart beat rising to a crescendo, Princess Hemangini didn't know quite how to respond to his statement. Three weeks from now! It was too soon. How could they organise a royal wedding in such a short span of time?

Immediately, her mind spun the other way. Or was it too long a wait before she became his? She shook her head, excitement and confusion warring within her.

"Hema... you do want to marry me, don't you?" A frown drew Devendra's brows together when he asked her the question. She had appeared keen enough the earlier day at the arbour. Then why was she shaking her head now?

Hemangini shook her head again, lifting a hand to stop Devendra when he would have spoken. "I apologise for confusing you, my prince. I promised to wed you yesterday and I will not go back on my word." She lifted her gaze up to his and gave him a soft smile. "It's just that three weeks seem too short a time to put a wedding together."

"Oh!" The frown disappeared from Devendra's forehead and he smiled right back at her. "I am sure Raja Brahmabatra and Rani Deepamala will be able to manage that. All you have to do is look beautiful." His voice softened to a mere whisper as he moved closer to her and said, "Believe me, three weeks is too long a wait to make you mine."

Hemangini didn't know where to look as the heat in the prince's gaze seemed to burn up her whole body with desire. It was a wonder that she didn't throw herself into his arms to be held close to his hard and muscular chest.

Taking a couple of deep breaths to steady her quivering nerves, she pouted at him, unable to deny his words, both about her parents organising the wedding swiftly and the wait seeming rather long for the bride and groom.

It was true that being the princess of the kingdom and the bride at this particular wedding, she wouldn't have to lift a finger. And yes, she planned to look beautiful. But for that, she needed to get her seamstress to make her a special set of garments. And then there was the jewellery. The ones she wore on a daily basis will not do for her wedding ceremony. They had to be really special. She pouted some more. It was all easy for the prince to say that everything could be organised speedily, but she wasn't really convinced about it.

"I need to talk to my mother," she said, turning right.

"Wait!" Devendra caught her hand in his. "You can't be leaving so fast. Shall we go riding? Or maybe to the garden like yesterday?" He gave her a mischievous smile, a dark eyebrow rising up in query, touching the lock of thick hair that had fallen on his broad forehead.

Her cheeks colouring a pretty pink of the same shade as her clothes, Hemangini shook her head. "There is too much to do, Deven. I have to…"

"I am not sure if Raja Brahmabatra would have read my father's message yet. Do you plan to go and declare to your mother that you are going to marry the Prince of Indrapuri? Just like that?" he asked, grinning at her.

Hemangini lifted a hand to place it on her forehead. "Oh dear! Good that you reminded me about that. It was so foolish of me. I had better wait for my mother to tell me what's going to happen." She paused, a finger on her chin as she wondered about how they should spend the day. "Do you want to go to the seashore? We can see the deep-sea divers in action and maybe ride on a fishing boat if the tide permits. Will that interest you?" she asked.

He nodded. "I would like that, especially if you are accompanying me." He took her hand in his, turning the palm up before pressing a kiss in the centre.

Dragging her mind to focus on the next course of action was extremely difficult for Hemangini. Pulling her hand out of his hold, she decided that they would go in one of the open carriages with the maids and guards riding in a separate carriage behind them. It was too difficult to keep her hands to herself as she itched to push back that tantalising lock of hair. Drawing a deep breath, she turned to Mahira who had been patiently waiting on one side along with Bahula and said, "Ask the stable master to get the royal carriage ready with the four grey horses immediately."

"I will, Your Highness," said Mahira, bowing low before swiftly walking towards the stables.

Turning to her maids—there were six of them today—the princess said, "Kamini, inform the queen that we are going to the seashore and will return later in the evening. Ask the chef to pack a basket with enough food and wine for all of us. We will have lunch at the beach."

"Yes, My Lady!" Kamini disappeared to follow her mistress's orders.

"The rest of you, get ready to leave in half an hour. Now go."

Bahula, noticing that everyone else had left to do their princess's bidding, quietly slipped away, leaving the prince and princess alone.

Devendra, who had been watching everything in amusement, took Hemangini's hand and pulled her into his chamber before she could blink her eyes. Shutting the door firmly, he gathered her luscious body against his own, his arms locking around her small waist. At last! He had her exactly where he wanted her, all alone.

"Deven…" Hemangini lifted her face up to his, a small frown on her neat forehead. Her expression turned soft, her frown disappearing when she noticed the errant lock still lying on his forehead. Lifting a hand, she gently pushed it back, her fingers tingling when they felt the soft and silky texture. So! Not every part of him was hard as iron.

She stopped midway, shocked by her bold behaviour. What if someone came looking for either of them? But seeing the desire in his dark brown gaze, she simply surrendered, laying her head on his muscular chest with a soft sigh. Of their own volition, her arms went around his waist, her breasts tingling as they pressed into his iron hard chest.

With a hand under her small chin, Devendra tilted Hemangini's face to his, looking into her shy gaze. "You look so beautiful Hema. I am so happy that you agreed to become my wife."

She bit her trembling lip, trying to bring some sort of sanity to the situation as her body desperately craved to become one with his. "You are a handsome and courageous prince, Deven. It will be an honour to be your wife."

"Hema…" He lowered his head, pressing his mouth to her luscious lips, tracing his tongue over their shape.

Hemangini felt the very ground shake beneath her feet as she felt his tongue probing deep within her mouth. She clung to his shoulders, rising on her toes to deepen the kiss. *Have I died and gone to heaven?*

It was a while before they came to their senses. Devendra lifted his head to study the wild colour on her cheeks, her lips having turned a dark red from his ministrations. Her breath was coming in gasps while her breasts rose and fell, the movement such a pleasure against his unyielding chest.

"Deven…" she sighed his name, "I think it is better we go before someone comes searching."

He sighed, removing his arms from around her with reluctance. Taking a step away from her, he gave her a nod, gesturing to her to walk ahead.

"Er… Deven…"

"What?" He looked her up and down with half-shut eyes, her taste still filling his mouth, making him crave for more.

She stood back. "Do you think someone will be able to guess that…?" She stopped, too shy to continue.

He smiled, lifting a hand to caress her cheek. "You look beautiful, as always. Well, your lips are redder than usual. But I think only I can see that because I kissed you. The others will not be able to notice the difference."

She wasn't so sure, but realised that they didn't have time to linger when she heard the sound of horses neighing as they led the carriage, the wooden wheels dragging noisily over the paved blocks in front of the king's palace. Giving him a glance from the corner of her eyes, Hemangini walked ahead to face her maids.

Kalpana and Kamini not only noticed her darkened lips but also the marks of fingers on her slender waist.

Walking close to the princess, Kalpana adjusted her *uttariya* in such a way that her waist was covered.

"What?" Hemangini gave her friend a mock glare.

Kalpana shook her head, a naughty grin on her face before she gave her princess a small wink, laughing when she saw the colour gushing into Hemangini's face.

When they reached the carriage, Devendra lifted the princess without an effort and placed her on the seat before climbing up to join her.

Hemangini was too conscious of his hard thigh pressing against her soft one. When she tried to move to one side, she wasn't really surprised when he simply moved closer, taking her hand in his hard grip.

Her prince will be an ardent lover, it seemed!

Moonlight Magic

They had a wonderful day at the seashore, what with the sumptuous food provided by Mahendrapuri's palace chef along with the delicious *madira*, the casks chilled in the waters of the sea; supplemented by the freshly caught and cooked crabs and prawns in rich sauces. The fisher folk entertained them with music and dance at twilight, a fire having been built in the centre to ward away the coolness of the evening. Everyone sat around the fire in concentric circles, highly entertained by the song and dance, the drums and pipes adding to the excitement in the air.

Once the sun had gloriously slipped below the horizon to call an end to the day, Hemangini turned her head to look at Prince Devendra who was sitting next to her on the luxurious carpet that was spread out on the sand. He hadn't let go of her hand from the time they had settled down to watch the performances. The thrumming sound of drum beat was in synchronisation with her heart beats which thundered away as twilight blanketed their surroundings. The sky was a kaleidoscope of yellow, orange, pink and red which were quickly fading into darkness, making the fire glow brightly. Soon, the many bamboo poles strategically placed around the shore came alive when torches were lit and placed in the brackets fitted on them. Without even aware of what she was doing, she rested her head on his strong shoulder and gave a deep sigh when his arm found its way around her waist.

Devendra was equally thrilled and aroused by her proximity. He had taken the princess's hand after lifting her down from the chariot and had retained it within his hold most of the time, only letting her go when they had their lunch. Just now, when he felt the weight of her head on his shoulder, he couldn't resist the opportunity to hold her close against his side. Grateful for the darkness, he turned his face to kiss her temple, breathing deeply of her unique perfume of sandalwood and incense. His hold tightened on her waist and he wasn't really surprised when he felt her squirm when his fingers came in contact with the underside of her right breast.

"Deven…" Hemangini murmured, not sure if she was protesting or encouraging him to explore further. Her swollen breasts were ready to burst out of the bustier, longing for his touch on them.

"My dear!" His response was a half-groan. Three weeks seemed such a long time to wait to make her his. But then, the warrior that he was, his patience knew no depths. Tapping on that well of patience, he sat up straight, taking his arm away from temptation.

"Deven!" Hemangini protested, her lavender eyes appearing a deep purple when she turned her accusing gaze to his. She missed the warmth of his touch as she felt the cool breeze caress her bare waist that had been in his grip a brief while ago.

He gave her a smile, his teeth gleaming in the darkness. "You are too much of a temptation, my love. And there's only so much I can resist." His voice was a soft whisper as he spoke into her ear, his breath teasing the tendrils of hair that had escaped from the knot. Without meaning to prolong his agony, Devendra traced the shape of her shell-like ear with the tip of his tongue, the darkness giving him the cover that he desperately needed just now.

Hemangini shuddered, her head tilting the other way as she gave him better access, thrilled when she felt his lips and tongue straying down her jaw to her neck. She gave a soft gasp when she felt him dragging his tongue repeatedly over the pulse that beat rapidly at the point her neck met her shoulder. It felt as if her whole body was on fire while the point of contact was only the tip of his tongue against her skin. She jumped when she felt the sharp bite of his teeth on her bare shoulder, trembling from the impact of his caress. A deep sigh vibrated through her body when she felt him administering to the area with his tongue, looking deeply into her eyes as he continued kissing his way down her arm.

She swiftly turned around to bury her face on his shoulder, uncaring of the people around them. But then, there were a number of couples who had separated themselves from the main crowd and were making love openly, the music and the sound of the waves along with the open fire adding to the romantic atmosphere.

Devendra turned her around to seat her on his thighs, his arms circling around her before he lifted his large hands to cup her breasts over her bustier, shocking her into silence as his thumbs drew lines above the cloth, pressing into her pliant flesh.

It all happened too fast. She had only meant to press her face to his chest. But now, she found herself seated on his lap, his hard thighs feeling wonderful against her lush buttocks. And his hands were wreaking havoc with her twin mounds as he squeezed them. Surprisingly, his touch was gentle as against his usually hard touch. It was probably because of the softness of her flesh. She didn't know, nor did she care as she savoured the way his hands moved over her flesh, the repeated brushing of his palms against her nipples making them go hard. She pressed herself closer into his hands, longing for more.

"Hema…"

She was startled when she felt the bite of his teeth on her earlobe, even as her heartbeat rose to a crescendo, and she lifted a hand to touch his manly cheek that felt rough with the growth of a day's beard. She wasn't sure what had happened to her earring, nor did she care as she rubbed her palm to his hard cheek before turning her head to press her mouth to his square chin.

Devendra bent his head to capture her teasing mouth with his, kissing her deeply, tangling his tongue with hers as he rocked her on his lap, his shaft hardening and thickening as his desire for making her his increased by the minute.

Taking a deep breath and gritting his teeth to bring some semblance of restraint to the desire that was blowing exceedingly out of control, he lifted her from his lap and placed her on the ground next to him.

A startled Hemangini, who had been in the throes of deep passion, opened her slumberous gaze to glare up at him, unaware of how she appeared with her bustier loosened, her hair coming out of its knot, with the jewellery on her hair all askew and one earring having disappeared.

To the man in front of her, she looked even more desirable than she had been a while ago. So much so, that he wanted to eat her up whole. Devendra got up from where he was sitting and walked away, unsure of what he might do if he continued to sit next to the princess. She was too innocent and deserved way more gentleness than what he thought he was capable of right now.

Feeling relieved that she didn't call out to him or follow him, Devendra walked along the seashore, the gentle waves having a calming effect as they caressed his bare feet, his leather shoes lying forgotten near the carpet where he had left the woman he had fallen in love with.

All this long, the Prince of Indrapuri had been sure that he desired the Princess of Mahendrapuri, more than any woman he had met in his young life. But just now, he knew that Hemangini was the light of his life and he would do anything to keep her happy and even lay his life down for her sake.

Yes, he loved her with the whole of his heart!

Princess Hemangini couldn't believe her eyes when she saw the prince suddenly get up and leave. One moment, she was seated on his lap and was at the receiving end of his passionate kisses. The next moment, she had been left on the carpet, bereft of his touch. What had gone wrong?

She felt hurt and angry and not a little ashamed. She surreptitiously looked around to see if people were watching her. But then, if anybody had witnessed their lovemaking, they all seemed to have turned away in the other direction, saving her a lot of embarrassment.

Her first instinct was to run behind Devendra and pick a quarrel with him. How dare he arouse her to a fever pitch and leave her so suddenly? Didn't he care at all for her feelings?

Taking deep breaths, Hemangini fought for control as her temper tried to break the bounds of decency. She wanted to scream and shout. But then, that would be a foolish thing to do. First of all, the prince was already out of hearing and all the noise she raised wouldn't affect him. And there was also the fact that she was the princess of this kingdom. She definitely didn't want to become a laughing stock and lose the respect the fisher folk had for her.

She searched around with desperate eyes and noticed Kamini sitting some feet away. Beckoning to her, the princess noticed that Kalpana wasn't to be seen, nor was Mahira. Somehow, Hemangini guessed that the two of them were attracted to each other. A bitter smile made the corners of her mouth droop. Weren't some people lucky to find love so easily!

Kamini walked over to the princess and gave her a smile and a wink. "Shall I help you straighten your clothes, My Lady? And I will have to set right your hair too. Oh, where's the earring on your right ear, My Princess? Have you lost it?" Not noticing the irritated expression on her mistress's face, Kamini ranted on and on.

"Keep quiet, Kamini. Yes, I need help with my clothes and hair. And no, I haven't lost my earring. Here it is!" She handed the *jhumka* to her maid, turning her face away.

Kamini finally realised that something was wrong. Realising that it wasn't the right time to question the princess, she quickly untied the knot of Hemangini's bustier and retied it firmly. Unpinning the *maang tikka* from the top of her head, she handed it to the princess. Taking a wooden comb from her silk *jhola* bag, she opened the intricate knot of hair at Hemangini's back and combed it thoroughly before deftly tying it up again. Kamini couldn't help but notice the red marks on the princess's neck and shoulder but refrained from commenting. The *maang tikka* was pinned back over the princess's forehead and hair parting before the *jhumka* was fixed on her ear.

Lifting the princess's chin to check her face in the firelight, Kamini nodded her head. "You look beautiful, as always, My Lady, though sad. Is something the matter?" While she had done her best to give the princess and prince some privacy in the darkness, she couldn't help but notice the way they had clung together. Also aware of the fact that the princess was deeply attracted to the prince, Kamini had expected to find her mistress happy instead of sad. But almost immediately, Kamini realised that the princess was not sad, but angry.

Her eyes welling with angry tears and her body protesting in frustration at being left dissatisfied, Princess Hemangini sniffed, doing her best to curb the tears from rolling down her face. Pressing her hands to her cheeks, Hemangini made a valiant effort to hold back her temper.

"My Lady! Shall I ask them to set up the chariot? Would you like to return to the palace and rest before dinner?" said Kamini, giving her mistress a shocked look. Hemangini was generally a happy person. She had never seen the princess in such a sorry state before now, not ever.

But then, Hemangini had never seen this side of herself either. Devendra seemed to have managed to plumb the depths of her passionate nature. Always a cheerful person, the princess had laughed her way through life all this long. But the past few days, her emotions had been in a constant state of tumult; joy, anger, desire, frustration and passion creating such an upheaval in her young heart while her body seemed to have woken up with a vengeance.

She shook her head at her maid. "No, Kamini. Rajkumar Devendra has gone for a walk along the beach. I would rather wait for him before going back home." She had some questions for him and she didn't plan to rest until he gave her the answers she sought.

The full moon was high up in the sky when Devendra finally returned to the place where he had left Hemangini.

"Are you ready to return home, Rajkumar Devendra?" asked Hemangini, her voice hoarse as she eyed him. He had removed his tunic, his bronzed shoulders and chest gleaming in the moonlight. She swallowed as she noticed the muscles in his arms and shoulders ripple with every movement of his. The princess had seen bare-chested warriors wrestling and sword fighting a number of times. But she had never been affected on those occasions, not even a little. Just now, she clenched her hands into fists as she watched Devendra bend down to strap his shoes on his broad feet, her throat choking up as desire rose sharply within her at the sight of him.

Devendra stood up straight to gaze down at Princess Hemangini with a small frown on his face. Why was she addressing him as Rajkumar Devendra? Hadn't they got over that formality some days ago? "Princess? Is everything alright?"

Noticing that Kamini had already gone to speak to the charioteer, and no one else was around, the princess pouted at the prince. "Nothing at all. Why do you ask?"

The perceptive prince noticed that her eyes were reddened. It wouldn't have been obvious in the moonlight unless one looked closely, which the prince did. Had she been crying?

"Hema? You were happy enough when I left you. I..."

"Do you really think so?" The words were out before Hemangini could stop herself, her anger rising to the fore once again. He had stopped making love to her so suddenly and simply walked away while she had been left feeling bereft, her body trembling with the lack of fulfilment of her desire. And he had the insolence to ask her if everything was alright. She felt a sudden urge to claw at him as she glared at the expanse of bare skin that made her quiver with need.

Devendra stared at the princess's lovely face, finally grasping that she was angry. Her eyes spewed fire at him while her luscious breasts, the ones he had held in his hands a while ago, rose up and down with every breath she took. Her small hands were clenched at her sides as if she was having a hard time holding herself back from causing injury. At that moment, he fell more in love with the passionate princess who stood tall before him, understanding that it was abject frustration that had made her angry. As for him, he had taken a long walk, the soothing breeze and gentle waves cooling down his ardour. But it looked like Hemangini was having a difficult time controlling her passion.

He smiled gently, stepping close to her and placing a hand under her small chin to tilt her face up to his. "Don't be angry, my princess. It won't be very long before we are married. Once we tie the knot, I will not leave you midway the way I did just now. I hope you understand that I was losing control over myself and that's the reason I left you abruptly. I did not mean to hurt you, my love."

Fiery colour drenched Hemangini's face when she heard his words. It was only too clear that he wanted her as much as she wanted him. Her temper disappearing in that moment, she gave him a small nod and a smile.

Devendra stared at her face glowing in the moonlight and leaned forward to place a kiss on her forehead. "My princess!" he declared.

The Wedding

Time appeared to race at the speed of a galloping horse as preparations for the wedding took place, the whole of Mahendrapuri bustling with activity. The capital city was decorated with a number of freshly cut plantain trees heavy with flowers containing burgeoning fruits within their petals which were tied to bamboo poles that were driven into the ground. Both the royal palaces—the king's as well as the queen's—were polished from ceiling to floor, the marble flooring and the brass chandeliers shining brilliantly. The carpets were dusted and aired while the multiple aromas of sweets and savouries wafting from the kitchens could be felt all the way in the gardens.

Guests arrived from the surrounding kingdoms, kings along with their queens, and attendants. There were a number of guesthouses, small palaces in themselves, that were placed at the disposal of the guests; wine and food served through all waking hours.

The royal seamstress hired a number of assistants to get the princess's trousseau ready along with a special set of garments for the queen.

Jaivardhan was thrilled when he was given leave from his classroom for two weeks so that he could take part in the festivities surrounding his sister's wedding.

Each evening, the maids entertained the illustrious royals of Mahendrapuri and the guests with their song and dance performances. The court jester was at his best, making everyone laugh until their bellies ached.

While showing his participation with great enthusiasm, Devendra couldn't wait for the morning of his wedding day to dawn. Was it his imagination or did Hemangini appear more and more beautiful with each passing day?

The most frustrating part of the waiting was that the couple had no private time to themselves what with so many guests gathered around and more coming in every day. His own parents, King Chandrabhan and Queen Kanchana Devi, arrived three days before the wedding, along with a large group of ministers, courtiers and servants. Devendra was glad to note that his father had not brought along his other queens. *Probably my mother had something to do with the decision,* thought the prince, smiling to himself.

From the beginning, he had taken a deep dislike to his father's other queens, thanks to the influence his mother had over him. Kanchana Devi had been jealous and angry when her husband brought home each of his other wives, Paromita, Suvarnarekha and Vaijayantimala. Each time he had tied the knot with another woman, Kanchana Devi had shrunk within herself, hating not only the woman but her husband too. She had felt betrayed and unloved. But not really having a say in it, she had lavished all her love and attention on her only son and had done her best to poison him against her husband's other wives.

Touching the feet of both his parents in turn, Devendra went with them to the sumptuous quarters allotted to the bridegroom's parents which was as luxurious as the king's palace itself. There was enough space to house at least five hundred people on the premises and was more than enough as the King of Indrapuri's party consisted of only about half the number.

Wandering gypsies and other tribes stopped at Mahendrapuri, keen to be a part of the wedding celebrations of the royal princess. They had made their camps around the edges of the kingdom, mostly along the beach and on the banks of the Bhima River that flowed through Mahendrapuri and further on into the sea.

The music these groups played around the camp fires they set up each evening could be heard all the way in the market. The whole marketplace wore a festive appearance as all the shopkeepers had cleaned and polished up their spaces making everything shine. The citizens were also in an upbeat mood what with the king and queen gifting everyone with a lot of clothes and jewellery for the upcoming celebration.

Minstrels and other performers came from all around the kingdom and its surrounding areas, entertaining the crowds in the market each evening. *Tharra*, a crude liquor produced from fermenting sugarcane and was popular among the citizens, flowed freely in the shops that sold them even as fights and arguments broke out when some of the people imbibed more than they could tolerate. Sentries were posted at strategic points to head off such fights though the king had left clear instructions that no one was to be arrested and sent to jail; and only to be headed off and sent to their homes. After all, it was a happy time and the rules were made more lenient than was usual.

The wedding day dawned. Princess Hemangini appeared calm on the outside. But within, she was a seething turmoil of excitement, nervousness and impatience. The whole process of getting ready for the wedding should have been an enthralling experience for such a beautiful young woman as the Princess of Mahendrapuri. But her eagerness to be with Prince Devendra overrode everything else.

Her wedding attire was truly gorgeous, what with the intricately woven silk skirt and bustier of creamy white with a red border heavily embroidered in gold thread in the design of swans. The *uttariya* was in red made of gossamer thin silk, letting one catch a glimpse of the sheen of the princess's shoulders which were a beautiful shade of ivory.

Her dark hair was braided into three plaits and then folded into an intricate knot to lie heavily at the back of her neck. The whole of her head was covered in gold ornaments inset with diamonds and rubies. The matching *maang tikka, jhumkas* and *nathni* covered her forehead, ears and one half of her face, giving the princess an alluringly mysterious appearance.

The *rani haar* that fell from her neck had seven strands of pearls ending in a diamond pendant that reached down to her abdomen while the *galobandh* that graced her throat was a beaten gold collar with a flower shaped pendant of rubies. Between the *rani haar* and *galobandh*, Kalpana placed a line of gold chains of different lengths and designs, one after the other.

"You look so beautiful, My Lady! The prince will not be able to take his eyes off you," said Kamini, giving her nervous princess an adoring smile. Amala nodded vigorously from where she was kneeling on the floor as she placed the golden *payal* around Hemangini's ankles even as Kamini clipped the matching pair of *bajubandh* shaped like coiled snakes with ruby eyes around her upper arms. The royal jeweller had surpassed himself while designing the jewellery for the princess's wedding.

Hemangini got up from the dressing stool so that Kalpana could pin the *kamarbandh* around her waist, the chains of gold beads falling in intricate downward arcs on both her hips, drawing attention to their slender shape.

Lastly, it was the turn of the many bangles and *kadas* to grace her slender wrists and rings for her fingers. Just then, the queen entered Hemangini's chamber. The maids moved to the side when the queen walked up to her daughter, studying her from the top of her head to the tips of her toes, her eyes shimmering with emotional tears. Cupping Hemangini's cheeks in both her hands, Deepamala spoke in a gruff voice, "You look so beautiful, my dear child. I only hope Rajkumar Devendra realises how blessed he is to have you as his *ardhangini*."

"Mother!" Hemangini reached forward to hug her mother, touched by the queen's words. That is exactly what she desired, to become Prince Devendra's other half.

It was a while before the mother and daughter could contain their emotions. Deepamala moved back to look at her elder born once again, a loving smile on her face. "It's time to go to the main hall, Hema. The Rajkumar is already waiting for you at the marriage *mandap* along with his family." Turning to the maids, the queen said, "Kalpana, Kamini, Amala, bring the princess to the *mandap* soon after I leave."

The maids bowed their heads, nodding their heads in unison. "Sure, Your Majesty. We will do that," they promised.

The two of them held Hemangini's hands and walked behind her along with Amala as they went to the court hall which was unrecognisable, what with the decoration of flowers and brightly lit oil lamps; people sitting on decorated chairs on one side while there were more of the guests seated on the carpets. At the far end, the area where the king usually held his court, a sacred fire had been lit. King Brahmabatra was seated on a raised platform on one side along with his relatives, ministers and courtiers; with Jaivardhan on his lap.

On the other side were King Chandrabhan and Queen Kanchana Devi with their people sitting right after them. Behind the sacred fire sat Prince Devendra, attired in a long tunic of gold silk, diamonds flashing at his ears and neck. A gold turban with a *sarpech* set with an uncut ruby the size of a pigeon's egg surrounded by smaller diamonds graced his head.

It was a wonder that no one noticed the impatience thrumming from within him as Devendra waited for his bride to show up. The music from the pipes and drums enhanced the pace of his heart when his gaze fell on Princess Hemangini who walked in just then through a doorway at the side. His breath stopped for a few moments before coming out in a soft gasp as he eyed her beautiful form appearing resplendent in the silk and gold that covered her from head to toes.

Her lips shone a deep red as she lifted her gaze to meet his eyes head on, the lavender eyes shining with joy and desire.

Tonight, she would be mine! The prince couldn't contain his excitement at the thought.

The princess was thinking the same as she slowly walked forward to sit next to the prince on the dais provided for the royal bride.

The pandit immediately started reciting the *mantras* while performing the rituals, not giving the prince and the princess an opportunity to talk to one another. But that didn't stop their eyes from holding a conversation as they eyed one another behind the smoke of the ritual fire.

Finally, it was time for the prince to place the *mangalsutra* around the princess's neck and the *sindoor* at the point where her forehead met her hair parting, making them both man and wife. Devendra took Hemangini's hand in a firm grip and gave her a small wink; thrilled to see the hot colour rushing up her face.

"You are mine!" he whispered in her ear, his brown eyes glinting possessively.

"As you are mine!" she responded, her lavender gaze glowing with mischief.

He laughed softly, pressing his thumb into her palm in acknowledgement.

Just then, Queen Kanchana Devi made an announcement which shocked the newly married couple no end. "We leave immediately after partaking the wedding lunch," the Queen of Indrapuri spoke loudly and clearly.

King Brahmabatra lifted his startled gaze to Kanchana Devi and then to King Chandrabhan as if for confirmation. "But, Your Majesty, it would be an honour if you could spend some more days in our kingdom," he said in a respectful voice.

Hemangini raised an eyebrow at her husband, as if to ask him why. Devendra gave a small shake of his head, unknowing of his mother's plans. He waited impatiently for her to respond to King Brahmabatra.

"That will not be possible, Raja Brahmabatra. We have to perform a *puja* at our *Kuldevi's* temple before the marriage can be consummated. I want to complete this ritual as soon as possible as I don't want the couple to stay apart for a longer time. I am sure you understand."

If the King or the Queen of Mahendrapuri was shocked or found Kanchana Devi's reply unpalatable, neither showed it in their expression. The king nodded, saying, "As you wish, Your Majesty. I will ask my men to pack all your belongings immediately." He turned and gave a nod to one of his ministers who went off to do the needful.

Devendra went forward to take his mother's hand, saying, "What is this, Mother? You never mentioned anything about the *Kuldevi puja* before now." His frustration at the delay in getting together with the woman he loved was eating into the prince.

Queen Kanchana Devi laughed at her son. For one who didn't share a passionate physical relationship with her husband—the very reason why her husband had married multiple times—it was difficult for the Queen of Indrapuri to understand that her son and daughter-in-law could feel disappointed at the turn of circumstances. She told her son, "That was remiss of me, Devendra. But let me tell you now. We leave immediately to travel to Indrapuri. Everything has already been arranged to conduct the *puja*. We just need to return to our palace and the *puja* may be performed the very next morning. You can bed Hemangini once that formality is completed."

King Chandrabhan shrugged his shoulders when his son turned to look at him. Devendra was ready to break something. The whole of the group returning to Indrapuri together will take them at least four days and nights. That was mainly because his mother, the queen, will be travelling by palanquin and not on horseback. For all he knew, even Hemangini would be travelling in a similar fashion. How exasperating was that! The courageous prince didn't feel brave enough to meet his wife's gaze. Under the circumstances, the passionate princess was bound to be as annoyed as he was if not more.

Just then, he felt a tug on his hand and turned to look at Hemangini. She gave him a mischievous smile followed by a wink, astounding the prince.

Wasn't Princess Hemangini angry under the circumstances?

Camping in Bhima Forest

evendra paced his tent restlessly, up and down, up and down. But for his mother's stipulation, this would have been his wedding night, the night when he would have made love to his beautiful and passionate wife.

At Queen Kanchana Devi's insistence, they had set out soon after the wedding feast, on their way to Indrapuri. After some hours of travelling—the queen in the finely carved palanquin and most of the others on horse; while the rest travelled by carriages with all the luggage. Princess Hemangini had put her foot down, insisting on riding Agni, much to Devendra's admiration. It was a rare few who dared to go against the Queen of Indrapuri's dictates.

Hemangini had been polite but firm. Smiling at her mother-in-law, she had said, "Thank you for providing me with a palanquin, Your Majesty. I am sure I will need it during the times I might tire of riding my horse. Just now, allow me to begin my journey to my new home on my horse." She had brought both her hands together, showing her respect to the older woman.

Unable to deny her daughter-in-law's reasonable and polite request, Kanchana Devi had given a small nod before climbing into her luxuriously appointed palanquin, leaning back on the cushions and shutting her eyes wearily. The wedding ceremony had worn her out completely.

Hemangini was only too happy when her husband of a few hours lifted her on to Agni's back and settled her comfortably in the saddle. "Do you need anything else, my princess?" he asked her softly.

She looked into his avid gaze and smiled before shaking her head. "Nothing, my prince. Shall we go?"

He had jumped on his horse and the two had ridden together. It had been pleasant enough as they chatted desultorily, Devendra pointing out the many attractions of the forest that bordered both their kingdoms. "You must be familiar with the area," he declared, turning his gaze to her profile.

"Yes. I have accompanied the palace hunters a number of times."

Many of the servants and guards had gone ahead to set up camp, the colourful royal tents spread in a clearing in the forest, not far from the Bhima River. The central tent, which was made from richly embroidered red velvet, belonged to the king and queen. There were two smaller tents on both sides, in a brilliant shade of blue. One was allotted for the prince and the other for the princess, effectively separating the newly wedded couple, much to their chagrin.

Devendra's face was red with temper when he got off his horse before lifting his wife down from hers. "I..."

She raised a hand and placed it over his mouth, stopping him from spewing out his anger. "My prince, please calm down. I have a plan," she said in a whisper.

The frown refused to leave his face as Devendra looked down at his princess, an eyebrow up in query.

"Have some patience," she said, patting his rough cheek before giving him a mischievous smile. Before he could gather his wits to respond to her, she was already walking in the direction of her own tent.

He stood there glaring at her for a few moments before walking towards the river and its inviting waters. Removing his clothes, he dived in and swam for a while, hoping to get rid of his resentment towards his mother's dictum, but not really succeeding.

What was Hemangini's plan? And how did she even hope to execute it? The queen had guaranteed they couldn't get too close to one another by ensuring that the bride and groom's tents were built far from one another and separated by the royal tent. And there were sentries posted everywhere.

It would have taken him no time to simply walk into his wife's tent and spend the night with her and not one of the sentries would have dared to stop their prince. But how could he do that without showing disrespect to his mother who was also the queen?

Devendra gnashed his teeth before stepping out of the river, taking the towel his valet Sanjaya held out to him and drying himself without uttering a word. The prince was well aware that Sanjaya was still displeased with him, all because the prince had disappeared from the forest while hunting and gone to stay at Mahendrapuri without taking his precious valet with him.

Sanjaya couldn't understand how the prince could manage to go about his daily ablutions and dressing himself without his valet's help. He had decided to show his vexation by going silent. Arriving at Mahendrapuri along with the royal party from

Indrapuri, Sanjaya had immediately taken over the prince's personal services, but had refused to utter a word to his master all these days except to greet him stiffly whenever they came face to face.

Just now, Devendra was only too glad to have the chatterbox valet remain silent, his mind preoccupied with his wife.

Wrapping the towel around his waist, the prince walked over to the back of his tent, entering it when one of the sentries lifted the back flap, and stepping directly into his sleeping quarters. Once Sanjaya helped him wear a simple cotton tunic and breeches, the prince submitted to his hair and beard being combed vigorously before walking into the living area of the tent and settling down against the cushions of a chair. Looking at Sanjaya, Devendra said, *"Ekant,"* indicating he wanted to be left alone.

Just as the valet took a step towards the entrance of the tent, a sentry walked in to bow low before the prince. "Their majesties, the king and queen, send their compliments and request your presence at the celebratory dinner in the royal tent, My Lord!" he said.

Devendra turned to glare at his valet as if it was all his fault. Sanjaya immediately turned to the sentry and said, "The Rajkumar seeks privacy. Now go away," he ordered, before bowing to Devendra and quickly stepping out of the tent, torn between his irritation with his master and his commiseration regarding the non-consummated marriage. By now, everyone in the royal party knew that the wedding night had been postponed for at least one whole week if not longer.

The prince looked around the living area, unimpressed by the cushioned chairs and tables groaning under the many silver plates holding a variety of fruits and a jug of *madira* along with some beautifully carved cups to drink it from. Lamps were lit all around, making the place appear almost as bright as day. He could also see camp fires lit outside while brightly burning torches shed light on the whole camp as people walked here and there as they carried platters of rice, cooked meats, vegetables and more, from the open cooking area to the royal tent.

If his mother was going to be disappointed in him, too bad. Devendra didn't want to see anyone or participate in what would turn out to be the celebration of his wedding. What was there to celebrate?

He stopped in his meandering when he heard Princess Hemangini's voice outside his tent.

"How dare you stop me from going in?" she snarled at the sentry who had placed his spear across the entrance and bowed his head, doing his best to show her that he meant no offence.

"I apologise, My Lady! Please understand that I mean no disrespect. But the prince doesn't want to be disturbed," he said in a choking voice, fearing for his life when he noted the angry glitter in the princess's eyes.

"That order must be for the others, you fool. Not for his bride. Now get out of my way," she said, stepping forward.

"Hema!" Devendra moved the curtain aside to call out to his wife. "The princess is right. But you make sure to keep the others out," he said, before taking her hand and pulling her inside his tent and into his arms. The next moment, he was kissing her deeply, all the hunger of the past few days gushing forth.

It was a long while before Hemangini could catch her breath, hanging on for dear life with her arms around his neck. She buried her blushing face in his shoulder, rubbing her cheek against him. It felt so good to have his arms crushing her to his hard body, his hands caressing her bare waist.

"I want to make love to you, my princess." Devendra's voice was a growl as he pressed his lips to the pulse in her neck.

Hemangini lifted her face to look up at him, laughing softly at his angry expression. Cupping a hard cheek in her hand, she said, "As I want to love you, my prince. But the Rani Maa has a valid reason for us not to consummate our marriage. She…" She stopped mid-sentence when he moved to stand apart from her.

"I don't find it amusing, Hema. The Rani Maa has no right to…"

She lifted a hand to press it over his mouth, shaking her head gently even as she pointed her gaze to the entrance of the tent. Placing a hand on his arm, she drew her husband further into the tent, talking in a pacifying tone, "Instead of being upset about the situation, why don't we get to know each other better during this period?"

He looked her up and down, his eyes drawn to her tumultuous breasts before running over the length of her body. His shaft had been throbbing with need from the day he had spent some private time at the arbour along with Hemangini. He was all set to burst with his need for her and here she was, standing in front of him, seemingly unperturbed.

"Deven…" Understanding his feelings only too well, Hemangini took his hand in hers before placing it over her heart, letting him feel its rapid beat. "It's not that I don't need you, my dear. See how my heart beats for you." She choked when she felt his hand squeezing her breast, her nipple tingling under his rough touch even as heat pooled between her thighs. "We won't go against your mother, but we still won't deny ourselves. I have a plan. I…" She couldn't carry on further when she felt his teeth graze against her shoulder.

"What?" he growled, tracing a path from her shoulder to her neck with his tongue.

"Deven, we have to go for dinner. The Raja and Rani are waiting."

"I don't want to go," he declared, kissing the corner of her mouth.

She stopped him when he would have kissed her lips by turning her head, a hand on his chest. "You don't plan to brood, not on our wedding day, my prince," she protested, laughter bubbling up her throat.

"Some wedding day this is turning out to be!" Placing a hand under her chin, he turned her face to his before kissing her deeply once again.

With a great effort, Hemangini dragged herself out of his arms to stand in front of him, giving him a mock glare. "Come with me, Deven. I promise you will not regret this night."

"How will I not? You don't realise, Hema. Being a young and innocent lady, you don't know the needs of a man." He took her hand in his and placed it against his manhood, intending to shock her into realising his need. She had to know it was no laughing matter.

Hemangini's breath caught in her throat when she felt his hard shaft through his breeches. Unable to resist, she moved her hand up and down, delighted when his flesh responded by growing bigger and harder. Her gaze turning slumberous as she repeatedly ran her hand over him, she revelled in the feel of his shape.

"Stop it, Hema," he growled, all of his body trembling with need.

"Don't you like my touch, my prince?" she whispered in his ear, pressing herself close to his chest.

His hand in her hair, he pulled her away from him to say, "Only too much. But we can't carry on like this."

She gave him a mysterious smile before letting go of him. "Come for dinner, my prince. I will meet you later in the night."

"You don't know my mother. She has placed sentries all around. You won't be able to come here to my tent without being discovered."

"You don't know *me*, my prince," said Hemangini, giving him a wink. Taking his hand, she moved towards the entrance of the tent. "Let's go have dinner. I am hungry."

He followed her, curious to know what her plans were.

The Queen's Gift

The dinner that evening was not a pleasant affair, what with Devendra in an angry mood and the king not really happy about the situation.

King Chandrabhan didn't care for the idea of keeping the married couple apart from each other. The king and queen rested for a brief while after reaching the camp. After that, he spoke to his eldest wife.

"Listen, Kanchana, I understand that the *Kuldevi puja* is important. But it's not right to ask the young couple to keep their hands off each other for a whole week after their marriage. No red-blooded male will want to adhere to such a condition. If I were in Devendra's position…"

"And I am glad you are not, Chandra," said the queen firmly as she gave her husband an angry look. It was rare when the two of them saw eye to eye on any matter. "You know very well how important the *puja* is. Even more important is the fact that the bride should be a virgin when this particular *puja* is being conducted. Or the whole of Indrapuri will incur the *Devi's* wrath," she declared maliciously. "Don't you remember how it was when we were married?"

"Naturally, I do. But then, we were married at the Indrapuri palace, with the *Kuldevi puja* conducted the same afternoon. We consummated our wedding the very same night, if you recall." The king said in a stern voice. "And you don't really believe that, do you Kanchana, that our kingdom will incur the *Devi's* wrath?" asked the king, giving her a bitter look. It was his father who had fixed his wedding to

Kanchana Devi, a princess from a northern kingdom. If Chandrabhan had met her first and had had an opportunity to get to know her, he would never have made her his queen. Kanchana Devi was totally self-centred and didn't care for anyone, not even the son she professed to love with all her heart. And more than all that, she was completely cold in bed, which was why Chandrabhan had been driven into marrying again. "God is merciful and not wrathful. Don't do this to the young ones. I..."

She shook her head vigorously. "I am not going to listen to you, Chandra. And I would advise you to keep quiet regarding this matter. They both are young. It will do them a lot of good to abstain. It will only improve their will power." With that parting shot, she left the sleeping area to her personal quarter in order to get ready for dinner.

The king and his son brooded over the dishes, not conversing much while the rest—Queen Kanchana Devi, Princess Hemangini and the ministers— chatted comfortably about their journey that day and the sumptuous dinner consisting of thirty different dishes. *Madira* flowed, of which Devendra imbibed the most. Or he would have, until he felt a soft touch on his arm. Turning, he found Hemangini gazing up at him. When she gave a small shake of her head, he placed the silver goblet of wine back on the table, not really caring that it was three-fourths full. If his wife didn't want him drunk, then he was going to listen to her. After all, it was she who was with a plan for tonight.

Queen Kanchana Devi watched this byplay and screwed up her face in resentment for a moment before making an effort to smile. What kind of magic had this girl—and that's what the Mahendrapuri princess was, a mere girl—woven over her son? Why did he have to stop drinking just because she placed a hand over his arm? Kanchana Devi felt threatened by the hold Devendra's wife had over him, already. Was the queen going to lose her son's attention too? The way she had lost her husband's? The queen couldn't stomach the idea.

Now, more than ever, she was determined to keep the couple apart. Well, the *Kuldevi puja* could be postponed for a period if the astrologer didn't approve of the date, couldn't it? After all, as the Queen of Indrapuri and mother of Devendra, the decision completely lay in Kanchana Devi's hands.

With that thought calming her down, she smiled at the gathering before continuing to eat with relish. As for her daughter-in-law, the queen refused to say more than was absolutely necessary. She planned to speak to Hemangini in private after the meal was over.

"Hemangini!" Everyone was up after the prolonged but sumptuous dinner when the queen addressed her daughter-in-law.

"Rani Maa!" Hemangini bowed her head to her husband's mother.

"Come along with me, my dear. I have something for you." Kanchana Devi swiftly walked towards her quarters, leaving the others in the dining section of the tent.

Not left with a choice, Hemangini gave her husband a long look before following in the queen's wake.

"*Ekant!*" The queen pronounced the moment she walked behind the curtain. Her maids immediately left the queen alone with the bride.

"Sit down, Hemangini," said the queen, giving the other woman a small smile. *Whatever did my son see in this girl?* Kanchana Devi sneered. She looks like a child. So many beautiful princesses would have stood in line to wed the Crown Prince of Indrapuri if he had only agreed to it. But Devendra had wanted to choose his own wife. And this... this girl was whom he had tied himself to. She couldn't believe that her son could be so foolish. But then, Devendra's father was also a fool when it came to women.

She walked to a trunk which was placed on a table and opened it with a small key that hung from a chain around her neck. Removing a jewellery box from it, the queen brought it over to the princess.

"These are my jewels. The ones my parents gave me, you know. I had saved them all for my son's bride." Opening the box, she showed the princess two sets of jewellery; one of diamonds and the other of sapphires. "Don't they look beautiful?"

Hemangini, who had remained silent so far, looked at the necklaces, bangles, earrings and more lying haphazardly within the jewel box. She was shocked that someone could keep precious jewellery in such a terrible manner. It looked as if the ornaments had remained in the box for very many years and had never been polished. As she looked some more, she saw a length of black hair curling around a *maang tikka,* nauseating her no end. Holding back a grimace, she said, "Yes, Your Majesty. They look beautiful."

"These are all for you, do you understand?" The queen gave her daughter-in-law a smile that didn't quite reach her eyes. "But I am not going to give them to you now. They will be yours on the day you deliver the heir to the illustrious kingdom of Indrapuri."

Hemangini felt relieved that she didn't have to wear them right now. She wouldn't want to touch them unless they were cleaned up thoroughly and polished too. Controlling a shudder, she gave her mother-in-law a tight smile. "I understand, Rani Maa."

"Good girl. And listen, my dear. It is very important that you remain a virgin until the *Kuldevi puja* is conducted. Devendra is a man and an impatient one at that. He might not be bothered about keeping up with customs. But you are the daughter-in-law of the family. I expect you to make sure that traditions are followed. Do you understand me?" The queen looked sharply at Hemangini's face which was completely drained of colour by now.

"Very well, Rani Maa. May I go now?" Hemangini got up from the stool she was sitting on. She felt smothered in the confines of her mother-in-law's quarters, listening to her instructions, not liking any of them. "I am tired after the long journey and would like to go to bed. If you will excuse me, Your Majesty?" Remembering at the last moment, the princess bowed her head to the queen.

"Naturally, my dear. Aren't you happy that you don't have to service your husband tonight?" The queen giggled, giving the younger woman a sly look.

Completely revolted, Hemangini walked swiftly out of the queen's chamber. It was an effort not to run away from Kanchana Devi's presence.

The Visitor at Midnight

evendra, who had been lying on the couch in his tent awaiting his wife, had almost gone to sleep when he heard whispers outside. Sitting up, he listened to a gruff voice talking to the sentry who was on night duty.

"I have a message for the prince from Princess Hemangini. And it's urgent," said the voice.

"You wait right here till I go and find out if the prince is awake," said the haughty sentry, looking the youth up and down suspiciously. The moustache he wore belonged to a man, but the face was that of a youth, the cheeks appearing soft like those of a child, or maybe even a woman. "But before I do that, tell me something. I have never seen you before today."

"I came with the bride's party and that's why you have not seen me before," said the youth, his eyes downcast.

"Wait here," insisted the sentry before turning to the entryway. He sincerely hoped that he wouldn't be thrown in prison for interrupting the prince's sleep. There was no telling with royalty. The only thing that reassured him was the fact that the oil lamps in the prince's chambers were still burning brightly.

"My Lord?" the sentry called out before taking a step forward.

Sanjaya came forward to talk to the sentry. "What is it, man? Can't you see it's very late? The moon is already halfway up in the sky. Why do you disturb the prince at this hour?" he asked in a furious whisper.

The tall sentry appeared to shrink in size right before the valet's eyes. "Pardon me, Lord Sanjaya." The sentries had taken to addressing the prince's valet as lord because of the airs he threw. And neither the prince nor Sanjaya had bothered to correct them. "But there's someone out here, wanting to meet the prince. The princess has a message to be delivered, he says."

Sanjaya gave a nod, without smiling. "Bring him to me."

The prince had taken his valet into confidence and had mentioned that the princess, his wife, would be visiting late at night, once most of the people in the camp had gone into slumber. Sanjaya's anger towards his master had disappeared like the mist at the advent of sunlight when the prince had made him his confidante and trusted him with a task that Devendra wouldn't dream of giving anyone else.

The youth stepped into the tent. Sanjaya turned and told the sentry, "You may go. I will see the messenger out when he has given the message to the prince."

The sentry bowed his head low before stepping out and continuing to stand guard outside Prince Devendra's tent.

"My Lady!" Sanjaya bowed low.

Hemangini almost choked with shock that the man had recognised her. Ignoring his greeting, she said, "I need to meet the prince. My Lady Princess Hemangini has sent a message for him that I will have to deliver personally." Dressed in a borrowed tunic and breeches, her long hair wrapped into a coarse turban and a moustache that was too big for her face, she continued to speak in a gruff voice.

Sanjaya had only recognised her because he knew Princess Hemangini planned to visit her husband late at night. Otherwise, he might have been thrown by the slight figure in men's clothes. He smiled now, not keen to upset his mistress. "Let me check if the prince is awake, my man."

"There's no need for that, Sanjaya. I am right here. You remain here and keep a watch for any intruders. I need my privacy more than ever." Devendra had got up from the couch to receive the visitor he had been eagerly awaiting.

"You need have no worries, My Lord! I will ensure no one disturbs you," said Sanjaya, bowing his head.

Hemangini turned her startled gaze from her husband to his valet and back again, her shock giving way to amusement once she realised that the prince's man, Sanjaya, knew about the late-night rendezvous; just as her maids Kalpana and Kamini did. After all, the princess couldn't have disguised herself as a man and left her tent without their help. Even now, Kalpana was lying on her bed, pretending to be the sleeping princess, just in case someone went over to check.

Devendra reached out for the princess's hand and drew her away to his sleeping quarters. "I like your moustache," he said, his eyes crinkling with laughter, wide awake now that his adorable wife was here to meet him.

Hemangini laughed before peeling it off her face. "Not as luxurious or beautiful as yours," she grinned, before saying, "I need to wash."

Devendra went to the corner of his room where a stand held a large brass vessel with water in it. Taking a wash cloth, he dipped it into the water and walking back to the princess, he gently wiped her face.

Her heart beat rose to a crescendo when she noticed the desire in her husband's dark gaze. "Deven…"

He threw the wash cloth over his shoulder before gathering her into his arms. "My love!"

Just when he bent down to kiss her, Hemangini placed a hand over his mouth, shaking her head slowly. "My prince, let us not forget the Rani Maa's condition."

He grimaced even as he gave her a nod. "If that's what you want."

"Deven!" She pouted at him. "It's not about what I want and you very well know that."

He took her hand in his before bending down once again to capture her mouth with his. Silence reigned for a long time as the prince explored her mouth, his tongue reaching out to caress the roof of her mouth, making her tremble with need. Copying his gesture, she returned the caress, and was thrilled to hear him groan. She placed her hands on his shoulders to hold on tight when he lifted her into his arms and carried her over to the bed. Her turban had fallen off by now and her hair flowed freely, spreading over the soft pillows filled with goose feathers.

He lay next to her, brushing his hand over her face in a rough caress. Smiling down at her, he growled, "Though the jewellery enhances your beauty, just now, I am glad that you aren't wearing any," before taking a soft earlobe between his teeth and stroking it with his tongue.

Hemangini lifted a hand to run it over his rough cheek, her eyes drawn to his handsome face. She raised her head to press her mouth to his, seeking his kiss.

Gathering her in his arms, Devendra obliged her, drawing her tongue into his mouth and sucking gently on it.

She pressed closer to the heat of his body, glad that he had removed his tunic by now, running her hands from shoulder to hip, revelling in the texture of his muscular chest sprinkled with dark hair. Pulling away from his kiss, she traced her mouth over the pulse at his neck, recalling the time he had caressed her in a similar way.

His breath came in gasps as he felt her soft mouth and tongue against his neck even as her small hands explored his chest. He smiled at his wife's boldness, completely enamoured by her caresses. Rising up on his elbows, he unknotted the rope that held the masculine tunic that Hemangini wore, lifting her body to pull her arms free from the garment. He stared at the bustier that was tied tightly across her luscious breasts, obviously in an attempt to pass her off for a male and smiled slowly as he lifted his gaze to her face.

Colour flooded the princess's cheeks when she felt her husband's eyes on her breasts. She so wanted him to touch her. She sat up to turn sideways and said in a shy whisper, "You will have to help me untie the knot."

"With pleasure, my princess," he said equally softly, before untying the complicated knot swiftly even though his hands were trembling with the desire heating his blood. Throwing the long piece of cloth down on the floor, he placed a hand on her shoulder to turn her around to face him once again, his eyes going wide when he saw the bounties in front of him, the nipples going tight and hard even as he watched her with his avid gaze. "Hema…" Reaching forward, he drew a forefinger over a tip before he joined his thumb to the finger to pluck at it gently, astounded by the colour that spread over her chest.

"Deven…" Hemangini moaned, her head thrown back, her eyes tightly shut and her hands pressed over the pillows at the back as she thrust her upper body closer to her husband.

He cupped her breasts in both his hands, squeezing them gently at first and then harder when he felt her enthusiastic response, rubbing his thumbs over the tips in a circular motion. "You look so beautiful, my love. Even more beautiful than I had imagined."

She opened her slumberous gaze to meet his heated one and gave him a soft smile that made his blood soar, his tumescent shaft pressing painfully against his breeches. Taking deep breaths, he did his best to ignore his body's demands before bending down to take a stiff nipple which was the colour of ripe peaches, into his mouth, rubbing his tongue over it again and again.

Hema sat straighter, lifting her hands from behind to hold his head in them as she pulled him nearer, even as she pressed closer to him, thrilled to feel his mouth widen and take more of her sensitive flesh within. Her hands ran through his silky locks and down his wide shoulders, her legs thrashing as she felt the heat rising in the core of her body. His hands and mouth at her breasts made her only crave for more. "Deven…"

He lifted his eyes to hers, his mouth still at her breast and smiled. "You taste wonderful, my love," he said before turning his head to suckle the other breast.

Hemangini was fascinated to see his dark head pressed against her pale body even as every nerve in her screamed with joy on one side and a deep need on the other. She ran her hands over his back, the strong muscles feeling as if they were iron encased in silk. When her hands encountered his breeches, she paused. Should she ask him to remove them? Will they be able to stop at the right time? Just now, the blood was soaring so wildly in her veins that she wasn't so sure. Oh yes, she did know what happened in the marriage bed, her mother having explained it all to her. And personally, she knew only too well what her body craved, for Devendra to move between her thighs, fitting his organ within her core.

Devendra buried his face in the crook of her scented neck, taking deep breaths to calm down his ardour. For one thing, he didn't want to shock his young wife; though she didn't seem all that shockable. He smiled at that thought. For another, it was up to him to ensure that he did not deflower her. As the older one, it was his responsibility.

"I want to see you, Deven, all of you," she spoke against his ear, her lips brushing gently over the shape before she took a sharp bite of his lobe, grinning when she heard his groan of need.

His manhood leaping at her gesture, Devendra got up to sit on the bed, his eyes drawn to her breasts, the tips having turned red under his caresses. Unable to resist, he reached over to pinch a nipple, grinning back at her, but not responding to her words.

"Deven… you heard me." The princess lifted a small fist to punch him on his muscular thigh, moving her legs from one side to the other, unable to bear the heat between her thighs.

"I don't think it's a good idea, my love," he groaned, gathering her into his arms and cradling her body against his chest. "You know the Rani Maa's condition. We can't…"

"And we won't." She moved her upper body against his chest, loving the feel of his rough chest brushing against her sensitised breasts. "I just want to see you." *And touch you…* She wasn't going to share that thought with him, yet. Moving back, she reached over to remove the knot tying his breeches.

Devendra watched her hands as they worked on the knot, too aroused to stop her. Oh, he would love to have those same hands touching his manhood, caressing him the way she had done earlier that day, only it had been over his breeches then. He accommodated her when she pulled his breeches down his waist, standing up to step out of the garment completely.

Hemangini stared in awe as her husband's manhood sprang free from his breeches. Her curiosity getting the better of her, she knelt on the bed to reach with both her hands and held him, savouring the feel of his organ as she caressed him from the root to the tip, again and again.

Devendra tilted his head back to groan, long and loud, his body shuddering in ecstasy. He had never felt like this, as if he would soon burst out of his skin, his heart palpitating at such a tremendous speed that he had never experienced before now. He thrust his lower body repeatedly even as she held his organ tightly between her two small hands and before long, he reached a powerful climax, his strong legs trembling with the experience. "Hema…" he moaned before falling on the bed beside her and burying his face in her breasts. "That was simply amazing, my love," he said in a hoarse voice, kissing her breast.

"Go to sleep, my prince," she said, running a caressing hand over his head. It had been a long while since she had come over to his tent. It was time she returned to hers.

"But I want to… I…" On the verge of sleep, the prince's voice slurred, his body satiated after the long and painful wait.

"Tomorrow, my love. Sleep now." She held him close, her arms around his back as she waited for his breathing to become even. Once she was sure that he was fast asleep, the princess slipped out from under him. It didn't take her long to tie her bustier around her breasts, wrap her hair into the turban and pull on her tunic before tying it in place. She quickly placed the moustache back under her nose. Checking herself in the mirror in the dim light of one lamp, she thrust her feet into her leather sandals before stepping out into the main section of the tent. Seeing Sanjaya deeply asleep on the floor near the entrance, she decided not to wake him up and walked out, her step bold.

The sentry lifted his hand in a salute when he saw the princess's messenger leaving the prince's tent. What must have been the message that it had taken the lad this long to deliver it? Mentally shrugging, the guard concluded that it was no business of his as he watched the youth walk away towards a camp fire.

Hemangini took a circuitous route around one of the camp fires, ignoring the men lolling around after having had a drink too many before walking to her tent. It was Mahira who was standing guard there. Having taken instructions from the princess's maid Kalpana—the woman he had fallen in love with—he had opted for guard duty on every night they spent in camp during their journey back home to Indrapuri. Without uttering a word, he brought his hands together in a gesture of obeisance before lifting the curtain to let the princess walk through.

Kamini roused Kalpana from the princess's bed and immediately changed the sheets and pillows, placing fresh ones for her mistress even as Kalpana helped Hemangini out of her male garb and into a loose robe. Smiling at her maids, the princess said, "You may both go to bed now."

She lay back on her bed, a smile on her lips, ignoring the throbbing between her legs, just happy that she had had an opportunity to bring pleasure to her prince.

Devendra was truly angry when his mother decided that they would continue in the camp for one more night before moving forward. "I am so tired after the wedding yesterday," she insisted.

Only that morning he had woken up with a smile on his face, his body remembering the way Hemangini had brought it satisfaction. He had told himself that it wouldn't be long when they reached home and the *puja* could be performed before he made complete love to his wife.

Was Queen Kanchana Devi deliberately keeping them apart from each other? A small doubt showed its head after hearing his mother's excuse for remaining back in the camp for another day.

They were having breakfast, the queen leaving soon after she had a drink of turmeric flavoured hot milk, announcing that she had a headache.

There was no smile on the king's face as he quietly munched on the beaten rice that had been cooked with vegetables and spices, asking his valet to serve him some *madira*. Under normal circumstances, Chandrabhan wouldn't have had the intoxicating wine this early in the day, but he was too irritated with his wife while being unable to do anything about it.

Devendra turned towards his wife when he felt her soft hand on his tense arm, the muscles bunched up. "Don't be angry, my prince."

"How can I not be?" he growled, a scowl on his face.

"Didn't you enjoy last night?" she asked, her lavender eyes dancing with mischief. She was so glad that she had outwitted the Queen of Indrapuri, who she found to be extremely malicious.

His frown disappeared to be replaced with a smile, his eyes glowing from the memory of the earlier night. "You were amazing, my love."

"I plan to meet you again tonight," she promised.

"I promise to make love to you, my princess. You will not leave my tent disappointed," he swore, his jaw tightening once again as he recalled his mother's unreasonable whim on remaining back at Bhima Forest.

"I look forward to it," she said, her throat choking with excitement.

"Would you like to go for a walk along the river?" he asked.

"Only when you finish your breakfast. You will need your strength if we are to carry on like last night," she said in a teasing voice.

Colour running over his clean-shaven cheeks, the prince gave her an amorous glance, eating his breakfast with relish as he looked forward to that night.

Hemangini held his heated gaze as she ate her way through the food even as she sipped on the herbal tea that Kamini had concocted especially for her.

That night, she made her way over to the prince's tent, after the moon had crossed its zenith in the sky. The sentry didn't bother to stop the princess's messenger, waving him in after greeting him with folded hands.

Sanjaya bowed to the princess, keeping his silence as she walked into the prince's bedchamber.

Devendra was sitting back on the bed, having removed his tunic. "Hema…"

"Deven…" She rushed to him and was thrilled to be gathered in his arms as he lifted her on to his lap before crushing her mouth in a deep kiss.

"Aah!" With a long sigh, Hemangini rubbed her cheek against his rough chest, her hand caressing his cheek. "Your cheek is not rough with beard," she exclaimed, lifting her face to look up at him.

He grinned. "I had Sanjaya shave me after dinner."

"Why?" she asked, looking into his gaze as she rubbed her palm over his cheek repeatedly.

"I don't want the bristles on my face to hurt your soft skin," he whispered in her ear, his tongue tracing the shape.

Hemangini whimpered in need when her husband slowly undressed her; first the turban, then her tunic and finally her breeches. "Deven…"

"It is my turn to pleasure you," he said, his mouth at her breast.

"You did pleasure me," she said before a gasp escaped her throat when he bit on her nipple gently. "Do that again," she ordered, gasping once again when he bit her a little harder this time before stroking it with his tongue. She could feel the wet pool between her legs and almost sprang up from the bed when she felt his large hand cupping her femininity. "Deven…"

"Do you like it?" he asked, stroking his tongue down her abdomen even as he gently pushed his forefinger into her core.

"I love it, Deven…" Her voice was a moan as she felt his finger stroking her wetness, thoroughly enjoying the caress even as her body craved for more. When he pulled his hand out, she growled, "Don't stop, Deven, please."

He laughed softly as he moved down to press his mouth to her core, then louder when he heard her shocked gasp.

"Deven?"

His hands caressing her soft thighs as he moved them apart, Devendra said, "Just relax, my love and feel it," before stroking his tongue over the seam of her core, making her moan, long and loud.

Gripping the silken cover on the bed with both her hands, Hemangini tried to calm down her palpitating heart that soared with each stroke of his tongue. Her hips lifted from the bed as she rose up to meet her husband's caresses, her body trembling as waves of shock built within her womb. "Deven…" Her head turned from side to side as she reached out for something, she knew not what, even as her husband sucked on her core, his lips and tongue pleasuring her relentlessly. Then suddenly, the waves that rose to a crescendo, broke apart, making her moan her satisfaction as the prince brought her to a tremendous climax that shook her to the very depths of her being.

Moving up to lie next to her, Devendra gathered her trembling body in his arms and held her close to his chest, his face buried in her neck as they went to sleep.

Hemangini somehow managed to wake up just before sunrise and getting dressed quickly, left her husband's tent, unaware of the silent figure following her at a distance.

The Princess's New Home

ight days had gone by after their wedding day when the marriage party finally entered the fortress kingdom of Indrapuri. Hemangini rode on Agni beside her husband who was seated on Vayu. She was impressed with the palace that was built on a hill, surrounded by a stone wall that was ten feet wide. Soldiers on watch were walking up and down when the *sringa*—a metal horn—was blown, announcing the arrival of the King, Queen, Prince and Princess along with those who had accompanied them.

A messenger had arrived the earlier evening to warn the royal household of the marriage party's arrival the next morning. There was barely enough time for the whole fortress to be decorated with mango leaves and colourful flower garlands, the people dressed in their best clothes to welcome their crown prince and his bride.

Just now, the three younger queens—Paromita, Suvarnarekha and Vaijayantimala—along with their children, waited at the entrance with a tray of *aarati* to welcome the newly married prince and his bride.

"Welcome to Indrapuri, Princess Hemangini," said Paromita, placing a hand on the bride's head in blessing. The other princes and princesses had gathered around to catch a glimpse of the bride.

Though Hemangini smiled at everyone, she wasn't sure who the three women were; the ones who were dressed in such silken finery and gold jewellery. She turned to look at her husband who bent down to touch their feet. Following his example, she did the same, trying to hide her confusion.

"Paromita, Suvarnarekha, Vaijayantimala," King Chandrabhan addressed his wives, "this is Hemangini, the Princess of Mahendrapuri who is now our Devendra's consort. You must all wish her well. And Hema, these are my other wives." He pointed to them as he uttered their names.

The colour drained from Hemangini's face when she realised that Devendra's mother was not the only queen, but there were three more. How was it possible that she had never known about this matter? Had her parents been aware of it? Her throat felt dried up while her hands trembled in shock. Why had no one told her that her husband had not one, but three step-mothers?

Would she have cancelled her alliance with Devendra if she had known this information before the wedding? Hemangini wasn't really sure. But she simply couldn't stomach the idea of a man having more than one wife. Why had King Chandrabhan married not one, nor two, but four women?

The root of her agitation was the worry that Devendra might go the same way as his father. Will she be able to tolerate it if Devendra brought home another wife? *I would rather kill myself than welcome another woman in my husband's life!*

Completely shaken by the discovery that her father-in-law had multiple wives, Hemangini lost both her colour and her smile; putting up with the formalities and greeting Devendra's step-brothers and sisters without really being aware of what she said to any of them. It was a relief when they walked into the cool hall of the palace and she could sit down in a chair, with Devendra beside her. More and more people came to be introduced and she must have said the right things as no one seemed to find anything amiss, but the Princess of Mahendrapuri was aghast at finding out what she had. While she was aware that it wasn't really out of the ordinary for men, especially from royal families, to marry more than one woman, it wasn't so common in her kingdom. Her father had set an example by having only one wife despite Deepamala giving birth to a daughter first. Her parents believed that a woman could rule a kingdom as well as a man, which is the reason why Brahmabatra had not felt the need to marry again to beget a son. That God had blessed them with a male child some years later was another story altogether.

But here in Indrapuri, the situation was very different, wasn't it? Queen Kanchana Devi had given King Chandrabhan a son and heir in the guise of Devendra. Why had the king married again and again after that? Hemangini felt as if she would faint with the way her mind revolved round and round the question. A deep fear roiled in her abdomen, that Devendra might do the same thing, not far into the future. Her heart beat harder than ever in her anxiety.

She turned her head when Devendra spoke to her, "Hema…"

"Hmm…" She refused to meet his gaze, not wanting him to read the expression in hers, one of betrayal. She felt herself on the verge of tears when her mind ran over the wonderful hours they had spent in each other's arms over the past few nights. While they had abided by Kanchana Devi's dictum not to consummate their wedding, the two of them had learned to pleasure each other without performing the ultimate act of penetration. She had learned so much about her own body, the pulsing nerve ends that reacted with such enthusiasm to his touch. The second night, Devendra had pleasured her the way she had helped him attain climax the earlier night. All the talk she had heard and the way her imagination had taken off—none of those had prepared her for the actual experience of coming apart in his arms at the caress of his long fingers and then his tongue within the core of her being. But… but…

She turned towards him when Devendra spoke to her again. "What?"

"You look pale, my dear." Which was an understatement. She appeared milky white. "I suppose you must be tired. Would you like to retire to our quarters for a while?"

She lifted heavy eyelids to look into his eyes which glowed with his love for her. *What will I do if he looked at another woman in the same way he is looking at me just now?* Hemangini wanted to scream in frustration and tear at her hair. She suddenly realised that she might want to claw out the eyes of any other woman Devendra looked at in a similar way. Such was her jealousy! And just now, a woman like that didn't even exist except in her imagination. She suddenly felt sorry for her mother-in-law. Had Kanchana Devi also felt angry, hurt and jealous when her husband brought home wife after wife?

"Hema..."

Suddenly, everything turned black while her heart weighed heavily in her chest. Just as she attempted to get up from her chair, Hemangini's head spun around in circles before she fainted, unaware of the strong arms that caught her before she fell down to the floor.

It was a long time before Hemangini opened her eyes and found herself lying on one side of a wide bed, Devendra sitting on a chair at her side holding her hand. Her eyelashes fluttering rapidly, she looked around the strange room, wondering where she was.

"Where am I?" she asked.

"In my chamber, which is also yours now," he said in a gentle voice, an adoring smile on his face as he brushed a hand over her forehead. "How are you feeling now? Would you like to have some water?"

She nodded, saying, "Yes," as she became aware of her dry throat. She refused to meet his eyes as she recalled the reason for her giddiness.

"Here." He placed an arm under her shoulders to lift her to a sitting position before holding a silver tumbler with cool water against her mouth. "Drink slowly," he said, concern in his voice.

She sipped the water, her gaze on his hand, the hand that had given her so much joy this past week. It was difficult to curb the sudden urge to scream as she pushed his hand away to sit up fully on the bed. "I want to be left alone," she said in a gruff voice.

Devendra looked at his wife, wondering what must have gone wrong. "Don't you like my family? Or maybe the palace? It is all new, I suppose. Give it some time and you will get used to everyone and everything." He was sure she was missing her parents and young brother and felt such a rush of love towards her. He swore to himself to make his wife happy; the woman who had given him so much happiness from the day he set eyes on her.

No! I will never get used to your kind of life; a life where a man brings home more than one wife. She wanted to scream the words at her husband, but Hemangini kept quiet, letting him believe that she was indeed missing her family. The truth was that in the excitement of beginning her new life with Devendra; planning and executing the secret visits she had made to his tent each night; she had had no time or opportunity to even think of her parents or brother.

There was a knock on the door before a footman announced the queen's arrival. Kanchana Devi walked into the chamber and went to sit on the chair Devendra had vacated.

The queen had a number of spies in her pay. She had ordered someone to inform her the moment Hemangini opened her eyes. And that's how she was here exactly at this moment.

"How are you feeling, Hema?" she asked in a stern voice.

Hemangini gave her mother-in-law a startled look, meeting her gaze boldly before saying, "I am alright, Rani Maa."

"I have told the *Raja Vaidya* to come and check up on you. He should be here soon," said Kanchana Devi.

"That will not be necessary, Rani Maa. There is nothing wrong with me."

"That is for the royal physician to decide. You are too young to know if something is wrong with you or not."

Hemangini's lips tightened, her eyes sparking with temper. "I have lived my life for seventeen summers. I know myself. Believe me when I say that there is nothing wrong with me." Her voice was firm when she spoke to the queen.

"There is nothing wrong if the physician examines you, right? What could be your objection?" asked the queen, eyeing her daughter-in-law with her shrewd eyes the exact shade of brown that her son had inherited.

There was a reason for the queen's interference. Her maid, Ratnamala, who had been keeping a lookout each night the royal party had halted in camp, had noticed the comings and goings from the bride's and bridegroom's tents. Ratnamala, always one to enjoy the intrigue that her mistress concocted whenever she could, had been only too excited to spy on the newlyweds. Despite all her efforts, it had been only on the second last night of the trip that she had discovered that it was not Princess Hemangini who was sleeping in her bed, but her maid. It hadn't taken her long to fathom that the youth who had walked into the princess's tent in the early hours of the morning just before sunrise, was none other than the princess herself. Ratnamala had got the rest of the story out of the sentry posted outside the prince's tent at nights. The man had been only too excited to share the details of the young messenger who visited Prince Devendra's tent night after night.

"I don't know why his messages take so long to be delivered. But then, it is the princess who keeps sending him to her husband. It is no business of mine to question him," he had told Ratnamala.

"Did you ask him why he was taking so long each night?" Ratnamala asked the sentry.

"No, no." The man shook his head vigorously. "I don't want to be thrown in prison. Lord Sanjaya always comes out to receive the messenger." He absolved himself of all knowledge.

So! The prince's valet was also in on the secret visits; just as Mahira who was guarding the princess's tent every night. Only, none of them had expected Queen Kanchana Devi's maid to sneak into the princess's tent from the back and check who was sleeping in Hemangini's bed.

Ratnamala had been too excited with her findings and had had a difficult time waiting for her mistress to wake up the next morning. The moment Queen Kanchana Devi was up, she walked into her chamber to say, "Your Majesty! It was a good thing you asked me to keep an eye on the couple. They have been spending their nights together, if not the whole, at least a part of each night."

Kanchana Devi was all set to burst into a tantrum, such was her anger. It took a lot of effort on Ratnamala's part to calm down her mistress. "Your Majesty! I have a suggestion."

"What?" asked the queen, her voice a snarl even as she turned her angry gaze on her maid. "It had better be good, Ratna. Or you might find yourself thrown out of here."

"Your Majesty!" Ratnamala brought both her hands together in obeisance. "Will I ever say something to displease you? Please give me but a few moments of your time and hear me out."

"Go on."

"Why don't you have the royal physician check Princess Hemangini once we reach home? He would be able to tell you if the princess is still a virgin or not."

The frown slowly disappeared from the queen's forehead as she pondered on her maid's words. "That's not a bad idea, Ratna; not at all." Kanchana Devi suddenly smiled at her maid. "Now I know why you have always been my favourite maid. I will do exactly as you suggest and call the *Raja Vaidya* soon after we reach Indrapuri. Now go and get someone to draw hot water for my bath," she said, dismissing Ratnamala.

It was an effort not to lose her temper with the queen, but Hemangini did make the valiant effort. The queen's suggestion was too annoying. The princess knew that there was nothing wrong with her and she really didn't care for the idea of the *Raja Vaidya*

of Indrapuri—a complete stranger—checking her for a non-existent illness. But how could she stop the queen from doing exactly what she wished?

Just now, she couldn't seek help from her husband. As far as Hemangini was concerned, Devendra was her enemy now. How could he have hidden the truth from her regarding his father having multiple wives? She was too angry with him to ask for his help in the matter of the physician's visit.

All I want is to be left alone! Hemangini wanted to scream as her temper rose higher and higher.

Devendra looked at his wife and couldn't believe his eyes when she refused to even turn in his direction. What could have gone wrong? He turned to his mother with a frown on his face.

"Mother!" When the queen turned to eye her son, he asked in a pacifying voice, "If Hema says she is alright, what is the need for the physician's visit?"

The queen gave him a malicious smile before looking at her daughter-in-law. "You both are aware that the *Kuldevi puja* is to be conducted tomorrow morning." She paused, waiting for either of them to say something.

Hemangini refused to respond to the queen's words. What was there to say? She had heard too many times about this *puja* and was rather impatient to have it done with as early as possible.

Devendra's frown grew deeper. "We are well aware of that, Mother. You have spoken about it a number of times since our wedding took place. What about it?" he asked impatiently.

"It is important that your wife Hemangini has retained her virginity until the *puja* is complete."

Devendra's face turned red with temper as he glared at his mother. "Are you saying that the *Raja Vaidya* is visiting to verify if Hemangini is a virgin or not?" he asked in an ominous voice.

Unlike him, Hemangini had gone pale, whatever little colour she had draining out her face completely. What kind of humiliation was this?! She couldn't believe that her mother-in-law, the Queen of Indrapuri, had the presumption to arrange for her virginity to be proved. How dare she?

"I will never allow this," said Hemangini, her voice the roar of a young lioness even as fury sparked from her eyes as she glared at the queen.

"I am the Queen of Indrapuri. You will abide by my orders," snarled Kanchana Devi, a triumphant look in her eyes as she glared right back at the younger woman. It felt so good to have such power over someone, at last. Even though she was the eldest consort, her husband, King Chandrabhan, had never let her have a say in the lives of his younger wives. And that had truly rankled, her pride taking a beating. Just now, the queen was enjoying herself tremendously, wielding her power over her son's wife.

But then, Hemangini was not a timid princess, not at all. She had always spoken her mind and had never been forced to do something that she did not care for.

Devendra spoke even before Hemangini could think of a fitting response to her mother-in-law's words. "Mother! That is unfair. You made a stipulation that my wife and I should not consummate our wedding and we have abided by that. You cannot humiliate Hemangini by getting the royal physician to check on her. I will never permit it, even if I have to go to the king for justice." Knowing his mother, he added the last few words to add emphasis to his view on the matter.

Hemangini felt her heart lighten when she heard her husband's words. Lighten a little, yes. But that didn't mean she had forgiven him for not telling her the truth about his step-mothers.

"Devendra!" The queen got up angrily to confront her son. "How dare you speak to me without respect? Especially in front of the wife you have known for such a short time? Do not forget that I am not just your mother, but the queen of this kingdom."

"Mother! This matter concerns not just Hemangini, but also me. I can vouch for the fact that my wife has not lost her virginity. You may stop the physician from visiting." He did not care for the idea of upsetting his wife. How could his mother make her feel so unwelcome on her first day in Indrapuri? Devendra had a good mind to ask his mother to leave his chamber so that he could spend some private time with his bride.

The queen gave a guttural laugh that sounded so evil to Hemangini. "Can you vouch for that, Devendra? Really? If you are saying that you haven't bedded your wife yet, I can only say I feel sorry for you. Maybe it wasn't you Hema had been visiting every night. But believe me when I tell you that your wife had visited someone each one of the nights we camped. Which is exactly the reason why I want the *Raja Vaidya* to find out the truth concerning her virginity."

Just for a moment, Hemangini's amused gaze clung to her husband's as joy and mirth exploded in her chest. She had had the best times of her life in those hours she had spent in the prince's tent each night. The triumph had been all the sweeter because of the clandestine nature of their meetings. She bit her lip to stop the laughter that gushed up her throat even as she lowered her gaze to the floor.

Devendra was absolutely pleased to see the mischief shining in his wife's lavender gaze when she stared into his. It had been for only a moment, but it had been enough to warm the cockles of his heart. Oh yes! Those nights had been blissful. He could not wait for this *puja* to get over before making Hemangini completely his.

But that was not the issue in hand. Just now, his mother, who had somehow got to know about Hemangini's nocturnal visits, was keen to have a physician test his wife's virginity. No one with self-respect, especially a princess of Hemangini's standing, would put up with such mortification. But it looked as if his mother was on a mission and nothing could stop her.

Before Devendra could respond to his mother, Hemangini spoke. "If that is what you believe, Rani Maa, then alright. Go ahead and have me examined. But I will not allow a man to conduct the test. Get a midwife if you will." She stood straight and proud in front of the Queen of Indrapuri, refusing to be cowed down. While she was also keen the queen became aware that the prince and princess had kept their promise despite all the temptation which had come their way.

Kanchana Devi stared at Princess Hemangini, unable to believe her ears. She had been so sure, goaded by her maid Ratnamala, that the young couple had consummated their marriage. How could her daughter-in-law so confidently agree to being examined? The queen was completely bewildered.

As for Devendra, he wasn't at all keen to have his wife undergo such indignity at his mother's hands. "You don't have to undergo this examination, Hema," he said softly, taking his wife's hand in his. "If what we did was wrong, then we should both deal with the issue together. I will not have you humiliated."

Hemangini took a deep breath. How was it possible to fall more in love with a man she was absolutely angry with? But no, it didn't matter. She wasn't going to forgive her husband so easily. "The man is always absolved in such a situation. It is the woman who has to suffer the shame. It doesn't matter. If the Rani Maa wants proof of my virginity, then that is exactly what I will give her." She tilted her pointed chin as she faced her mother-in-law courageously. "But not at the hands of the *Raja Vaidya*," she added.

Not really having a choice, the queen called for a guard to send the physician on his way before ordering another man to go fetch the oldest and most experienced midwife who lived in the same compound as the queens' palace.

The woman came within the hour. While the queen and an ominously silent Devendra waited in the next chamber, the old woman tested the princess. The proud Hemangini lay on the bed, a small smile on her face. She actually was eager to see the disappointment on the queen's face when the midwife pronounced Hemangini a virgin.

When the woman would have left her to go to the other chamber after completing the test, Hemangini stopped her. "Wait! Let me go with you." She got out of the bed to adjust her clothes.

The midwife bowed her head respectfully. After all, the queen's suspicions had been proved unnecessary. The Princess of Mahendrapuri was a virgin. Walking behind the new bride, the midwife entered the other chamber to bow low before the queen and prince.

"What is it, Kanaka?" asked the queen.

"Your Majesty!" Kanaka brought both her hands together in obeisance. "The princess is pure and untouched."

Devendra looked across at his wife, sure that she must be angry, but was startled to see a wide smile on Hemangini's face.

As far as the princess was concerned, these small problems did not matter. She would rather deal with bigger issues, such as the matter of multiple wives.

Hemangini bided her time before speaking to her husband the next night—their wedding night—about all her fears.

Kuldevi Puja

evendra couldn't help staring at the vision that walked out of the queens' palace that morning. He had been waiting for Princess Hemangini, to escort her to the *Kuldevi* temple in his chariot. The others, the king, all his queens, the other princes and princesses had all left for the temple by now.

When Kanchana Devi offered to wait back with him, Devendra had firmly told his mother to go along with King Chandrabhan. He so needed the private time with his wife.

The earlier day, Hemangini had been taken to the queens' quarters and was given a room to stay in, much to Devendra's disappointment. He had been keen that she spend time in his suite, but then the queen had been adamant that her daughter-in-law was to stay with the womenfolk of the royal family.

He gazed adoringly at his wife who was wearing a silk *antariya* and bustier of brilliant yellow, a matching *uttariya* gracing her shoulders; as if the sunshine had melted itself to be woven into garments especially for her. Diamonds glittered from the top of her head down to her ankles and Devendra was thrilled to see that she was wearing the set of jewellery he had sent over to her early that morning.

"Good morning, my love! Did you sleep well?"

Hemangini gave him a nod without lifting her gaze to his. "Good morning, Prince Devendra! I did, yes." Which was a white lie! She didn't mention that she had had an almost sleepless night; the first time in the past week when she hadn't been held in his arms.

Devendra frowned. There it was! Her formal greeting. It was obvious that she was still upset with him about something. He was yet to discover the cause of it; which was one of the reasons he had insisted on travelling alone with her. He lifted her into his arms and held her against his heart for a few seconds before placing her in the chariot.

Hemangini's heart was in her throat, on the verge of choking her as she felt his muscular arms gathering her close to his chest; so much so that she could feel the beat of his heart through the silk tunic that he was wearing. It was a supreme effort not to simply melt into his arms and forget the very existence of everyone else. But how could she do that? The others did exist and it was time they left for the temple as the *puja* could not begin without the newly wed bride and groom.

The prince stepped into the chariot and sat beside her, his muscular thigh touching her slender one when he took her hand firmly in his while the charioteer set off at a steady pace, the sound of the horses' hooves keeping time with the beat of his heart.

Hemangini felt desperate to move to one side of the chariot, but she knew for a fact that her husband would simply move closer. And who could blame him? Hadn't they shared such intimacy during the past few nights? Even thinking about those times in his arms, brought hot colour to her soft cheeks.

Devendra eyed his wife, wondering at the heat in her face. Without saying anything, he leaned across to kiss her cheek.

Lifting a hand, she placed it over his mouth to stop him from kissing her further. "You forget that we are going to the temple."

"That we are," he responded, holding her hand against his mouth and kissing her palm, brushing against the centre with the tip of his tongue.

Hemangini trembled with the desire that flamed through her veins when she felt the briefest of his touch on her palm. Her heartbeat soared even as beads of perspiration gathered on her forehead and upper lip. "Devendra!"

He shook his head. "That's not what you always call me," he said, looking at her expectantly.

"It is, after all, your name," she said, turning to look out from her side as the trees appeared to rush the other way when the chariot gained speed on the even track.

"Hema…" He placed a hand under her chin and turned her face towards his. "What is wrong? Have I upset you in some way?"

Though her face was turned towards him, her gaze was on the floor of the chariot, her eyelashes fluttering over her soft cheeks. She bit her lip hard, not wanting to talk about what was bothering her. Not now, not on their way to the temple.

"How will I know if you don't tell me?" he asked, leaning forward to trace the shape of her eyebrow with his lips.

"No, Devendra!" She tried to move away only to find herself within the circle of his arms. By now, he was so used to her soft and slender body that he was careful enough not to crush her in his iron hold, but had learned to be more gentle. Though Hemangini wouldn't have minded if his arms turned into bands of iron; as her softness so craved his hardness.

God in heaven! What am I thinking? Hemangini stopped herself in time before slapping her forehead. She didn't want Devendra's arms around her, gentle or otherwise. Placing her hands on his broad chest, she tried to push him away, only it felt as if she was trying to move a huge rock uphill. "Let me go," she said, her voice a hoarse whisper.

"It will take us a while to reach the temple. I want to simply hold you, my love." His voice was a gentle whisper in her ear.

That morning, Hemangini had been reluctant to open the jewellery box Kalpana had carried into her chamber. "Mahira brought this, My Lady! It is a gift for you from the prince," said Kalpana, handing the jewellery box to her mistress.

"Leave it on the dressing table," said Hemangini.

"My Lady, don't you want to see what your prince has sent you?" asked Kalpana, feeling extremely curious. It was a large box and must obviously contain something precious.

Recalling the box of unpolished jewellery that Queen Kanchana Devi had shown her, the princess wasn't too impressed. Just now, she was too angry with everyone in the royal family of Indrapuri, even her husband. She glared at her maid before saying sarcastically, "Why don't you open the box and find out? I can see that you are dying to know what it contains."

"No, My Lady!" Kamini, who had been setting out the princess's garments for the temple visit, protested loudly in a startled voice. "How can Kalpana open the box that has been sent to you by your husband? It is only right that you open the box, My Lady. It looks like the prince has gifted you with jewellery. Maybe your lord expects you to wear them today."

With a grimace, Hemangini walked to her dressing table to open the intricately carved ivory box. That she was angry with Devendra was something she hadn't shared with anyone, not even the maids who were also her friends. They would find it strange if she ignored her husband's gift. With a deep sigh that shuddered through her being, she lifted the lid, her eyes going wide when they fell on the gold choker that glittered brilliantly with diamonds, the centre stone as big as her thumb nail. She lifted the ivory tray that held the necklace to find a multi-layered *rani haar* with a side pendant, also of diamonds, below it. A third tray contained diamond *jhumkas* and a matching *nathni*. Two more trays held a *maang tikka*, armlets, anklets and *kadas*.

Despite herself, the princess was overwhelmed by the gift her husband had sent her. She was aware of his love for her and she couldn't help but recall the nights during their travel, wonderful nights that she had spent in his arms. But... but, she sighed, closing her eyes wearily. What will happen when he became attracted to another woman? She opened her eyes to glare at her image in the mirror. She would never tolerate that.

How much ever she tried, Hemangini couldn't persuade Devendra to let go of her. Tired of fighting him, she buried her face in his chest and shut her eyes, hoping that they would reach the temple soon.

She gave a sigh of relief when the chariot stopped at the foot of a hillock, not much later. Moving out of Devendra's arms—he let her go, finally—she looked up to see the temple tower on top of the hill.

Devendra jumped down from the chariot to lift her down before taking her hand in his and guiding her towards the rough set of stairs cut into the rock that formed the hill. It was still dark when they climbed the fifty-five steep steps in all and reached the entrance to the temple. The compound was large and despite the early hour, was crowded with people who had come over to participate in the special *puja* organised by the royal family that day.

Everyone moved to the sides to give way to their prince and princess, Devendra lifted his right hand in a wave as he looked to the left and to the right, smiling at everyone. He held Hemangini's right hand in his left as they walked towards the sanctorum. The princess also gave a shy smile as she looked at the citizens of Indrapuri, the kingdom she had embraced as her own; not showing the turbulence churning within her.

They walked into the sanctorum and saw the royal family standing outside the inner sanctorum. Queen Kanchana Devi had been watching out for the couple and gestured for them to go forward.

The ritual began immediately with four *pandits* chanting *mantras*, while a fifth one offered flowers at the deity's feet at the end of each thread of chant.

Hemangini stared at the granite idol of Triumbaka, consort of Lord Shiva, and felt the grace flowing into her even as she brought her hands together in prayer. She felt a powerful feeling of peace stealing into her as she stared at the beautifully carved idol in a standing posture, wrapped in a leaf green sari with a red border, embroidered heavily in gold thread. A circle of red vermilion shone on the Devi's forehead while a gold crown and other jewellery graced her person. There were brass oil lamps hanging from the ceiling; six on each side of the deity. The light from the lamps made the deity appear truly bright and beautiful. The pleasing aroma of incense teased her nostrils as she gazed mesmerised at the idol of the *Devi*.

The chanting went on for a while, the younger princes and princesses growing restless. Then, it was time for the *aarati*, with brass bells clanging loudly. One of the pandits brought the *aarati* tray out and showed it to the king first before walking down the long line of people from the royal family.

Everyone stepped out to perform three perambulations around the sanctorum before reaching the front and prostrating ahead of the tall flag pole directly in front of the sanctum.

Hemangini stood up to shut her eyes in prayer for a while longer. "Triumbaka, please set right my relationship with my husband and his family. Just now, I am too angry to want to remain here in Indrapuri. I fear that Deven will want to marry more women in the future, just like his father. Please help me, Devi. Bless me that I should remain Deven's only wife." She muttered the prayer in her mind before going on her knees to prostrate before the Goddess once again.

Devendra stood beside her, watching his wife as she prayed, her face glowing in the light of the rising sun, vying with the twinkling diamonds which graced her body. He wondered what she was praying for. With a soft smile on his face, he brought his hands together and muttered his own prayers. "Devi, please bless my wife, Hemangini and answer her prayers, whatever she wishes for."

When he opened his eyes, he found himself looking into Hemangini's lavender gaze and gave her a brilliant smile. "Shall we leave, my princess?" he asked her.

For a moment there, she had forgotten to hold on to her anger towards him. Meeting his gaze had made her anger crumble to dust even as colour rose up her cheeks. Lowering her gaze, this time due to shyness, she gave him a small nod. "Yes."

He took her hand in his as they walked down the stairs to get to their chariot. Devendra was keen to leave before any of his step-brothers or sisters insisted on joining them and was glad when the chariot took off before the others could reach the bottom of the hill.

The Wedding Night

Hemangini so wanted to hate all of Devendra's three step-mothers. But somehow, she found it impossible as they fluttered around her, helping her get ready for her wedding night. None of the three, Paromita, Suvarnarekha or Vaijayantimala, seemed to have even one malicious intent in her.

"I must say that our Devendra is truly lucky to find such a beauty for his wife," said Paromita, hooking the necklace at Hemangini's nape.

"Why ever not? Devendra is so handsome, maybe the handsomest in our whole kingdom, that he deserves nothing less," said Suvarnarekha, plaiting Hemangini's thick and long hair into three braids at her back. "I am sure you realise how lucky you are, Hema."

Colour rushed up Hemangini's face as she listened to the three queens who had taken over the duties of her maids for the evening while Kalpana and Kamini stood back to watch their mistress being decked with jewellery, though lesser than was usual.

"I would say that theirs is a match made in heaven. I feel as if Lord Rama and his Sita are walking towards me when Devendra and Hemangini walk together." This was Vaijayantimala.

The chatter continued through the whole time they got the princess ready for her bridal bed, not seeming to expect Hemangini to take part in the conversation.

Paromita stepped back to hold Hemangini's face between her hands. "You are perfection itself, my child.

Go now. Your husband must be growing impatient, waiting for you," she said with a wide smile.

They laughed when colour bloomed once again on Hemangini's face as she desperately turned to her maids.

Kalpana and Kamini stepped forward to take the princess's hands in theirs, leading her out of the queens' palace. "Have you moved my things to the prince's chambers?" asked Hemangini in a whisper.

"Yes. We could do it only because of the prince's intervention," said Kalpana, rolling her eyes.

"I don't know what you mean." Hemangini frowned at her maid.

Kalpana began to say, "Er... My Lady!" She stopped, hesitating to carry tales about the queen of the region.

Kalpana didn't feel such qualms. After all, their loyalty was to their princess. "The Rani Maa didn't want you to move to the prince's chambers. She insisted that you should live in the queens' palace."

"Is that where all the royal women live in Indrapuri?" asked Hemangini with a frown. Back home in Mahendrapuri, there was a separate palace for the queen. But that was just for the sake of it. Her father conducted his court in the king's palace while the kitchen and dining hall were also situated there.

Otherwise, King Brahmabatra lived in the queen's palace. In fact, both her parents lived in the same quarters. But it appeared that Indrapuri had some strange rules.

"Yes, My Lady!" said Kamini. "All the women and young children live in the queens' palace. The older princes live in the king's palace."

No wonder the king married more than one queen! Hemangini thought to herself. "How did the prince convince his mother?"

"We don't really know. When we asked some men to move your trunks, the queen sent word insisting that we stop and you are to live in the queens' palace. Sometime later, the prince sent his men to have all your things shifted to his chambers."

Hemangini gave a long sigh. While she was still piqued with Devendra for not telling her about his step-mothers, she would rather live in his quarters than live amongst so many women. Spending a little more than one day in their company had convinced her that they all led an idle life and loved to gossip. She gave a mental shudder as she imagined living with them. She would wither away because of the languorous lifestyle.

"I am glad. I hope you both have also been allotted quarters near me."

They nodded as one. "Yes, My Lady!" said Kamini.

Kalpana giggled, colour running up her face.

"What?" asked the princess, looking her up and down.

"Mahira's quarter isn't all that far away. That's why she's so excited," said Kamini, grinning.

"Oh!" Hemangini went silent, feeling envious of her maid's simple life. She didn't think Mahira would care if Kalpana gave him a son or a daughter or even if she didn't give him a child at all. Wasn't she lucky! Holding back the sigh that rose within her chest, she stepped into Devendra's chambers, forgetting her maids altogether when her gaze fell on her waiting husband.

Devendra wore a silk *antariya* and not much else other than the sacred thread which fell from his left shoulder down to the right side of his hip. He greeted her with a wide smile on his face even as his brown eyes glinted with desire. "At last! Welcome, my love!" He took her hands in his as he ran his gaze over her, his body tightening with need as he took in her beauty.

Hemangini bit her lip, gazing down at the floor, her eyes falling on his bare feet, the feet she had caressed over and over the last time she had spent half a night with him. Heat gushed into her face as she recalled the joy of being in his arms.

Guessing where her thoughts were taking her, he pulled her closer, lifting her hands to place them on his shoulders before clasping his own around her small waist. "Are you going to tell me why you are angry with me?" he asked, his mouth against her ear.

Hemangini turned her head to one side as she felt his lips whisper over her ear before seeking the vein at the joining of her neck and shoulder. Her hands seemed to take on a life of their own as they gripped his shoulders, rejoicing in the feel of the hard muscles sheathed in smooth skin.

"Help me with your jewellery, Hema," said Devendra in a desperate voice. They were getting in the way as he tried to caress her silky skin.

With a soft sigh, she slipped out of her husband's arms and went to sit on an ornately carved velvet cushioned stool in front of a floor-to-ceiling mirror in his dressing room. Lifting her hands, she unhooked her earrings, staring at his reflection as he came to stand beside her, still refusing to meet his gaze. She looked at her reflection and was glad that she wore way less jewellery than usual. Otherwise, it would have been a difficult task, removing the lot without the assistance of at least one of her maids.

"Here, let me help you," said Devendra, draping her braids on her shoulders before unhooking her necklace. Placing his hands on her shoulders, he gently massaged them, looking at her face in the mirror. He was disappointed when he found her eyes closed, her eyelashes spread like fans on her cheeks. "Hema…"

"Mmm…" She kept her eyes shut as tears gathered in them. The matter of his father's other wives stood like a wall between them, or that's how it seemed to her. Always used to speaking her mind, she had to control herself from blurting it out as she didn't know how Devendra would react if she asked him about it.

"My love!" He lifted her from the stool and made her stand in front of him, his hands gripping her shoulders firmly. "I know you are upset about something. Unless you tell me what the problem is, how do you expect me to solve it?" he asked. When she didn't answer immediately, he asked, "Would you like to have some *madira*?" Maybe the wine will calm her down enough to help her open up to him about what was bothering her.

She shook her head. No, she needed a clear mind and wine will only addle it. "No."

"Would you like to go for a walk in the garden?" he asked. While he wanted to make love to her, Devendra was clear he wanted a willing woman in his arms, not one who refused to even meet his gaze. Something had happened between the last night they spent in camp and the morning they reached Indrapuri. Had someone behaved badly? Insulted her? Even if they had, why should she be angry with him?

Snaking an arm around her waist, he walked with her to the back of his chamber from where they reached a veranda that led them out into the garden. The stars shone brightly while a waning moon rode over the skies. Drawing a deep breath as he took in the aroma of jasmine that came from the many creepers spread over iron railings, Devendra walked on the curving path that went around the palace, matching his strides to her shorter ones.

Hemangini tried to move out from his hold and when she didn't succeed, she simply gave in, leaning her head on his arm. She breathed in the silence and was glad that there was no one about.

"Hema?" He turned to press his lips to the top of her head. "Why don't you tell me what's troubling you?"

With a huge sigh shuddering through her whole body, Hemangini spoke in a trembling voice. "Your father, the king, has many wives."

He bent his head down close to her to catch her words. Hearing them, he responded, "That's true," wondering why she was stating something that was obvious.

"Why did he marry other women when he was already married to your mother?" She stopped in mid-stride to face him.

Devendra shrugged, studying her face in the moonlight. "I have never thought of asking my father that. And I think only he can answer your question. But why does that matter to you? I don't think you should mind if my mother and step-mothers don't."

She shook her head, biting her lip, not knowing how to explain her fears to him. "Devendra, I… you…"

The prince frowned. It was so unlike his princess to hesitate in speaking her mind. Something was obviously troubling her really badly. But it looked like she didn't know how to put it into words. Why would it upset her that his father was married to four women? His brow cleared almost immediately as he snapped his fingers, the sound echoing in the silence. Was she may be worried that he might want to get married again? Is that what had upset her?

"Hema?"

"Mmm…"

He placed a finger under her chin to lift her face up to his. "Are you worried that I might also marry other women the same way as my father? Is that why you are angry with me?"

Hemangini lifted heavy eyelids to look into his shrewd gaze before looking down almost immediately. Would he be angry if she agreed? But then, used to being honest, she didn't know how not to be. She gave him a small nod, "Yes."

"My love!" He gathered her into his arms. "Don't you know that I love you more than my life itself? I swear I will never look at another woman the way I see you. There is no need for you to fear that I will marry again. I give you my word that I will never do it."

Hemangini's heart beat loudly in her chest. She liked the words he spoke, but she wasn't convinced. Today, he was in love with her. What about five years later? Or what will happen if she wasn't able to give him a son? An heir? Will he still be of the same mind under those circumstances?

"Hema? I have a feeling that you don't know if you can trust me in this," said the intelligent prince, reading her silence correctly. "Don't you love me?"

She lifted her face to glare up at him. "You know I love you. And I have told you that so many times. How can you doubt it?" Tears trembled at the edge of her lashes before one rolled down her left cheek.

He laughed softly, before reaching forward to press a kiss to her forehead, even as he wiped her tear with his hand. "Will you marry another man if I don't give you a son?" he asked.

"What nonsense!" She almost shouted the words at him. "You know I'll never do that."

"Then, do you doubt my love for you, maybe? Is that why you think that I might marry again?"

She shook her head vigorously. "It is accepted in your family, that a man can wed many times."

He sighed, able to understand her argument. And however much he told her that he wouldn't do it, she didn't know him well enough to trust him completely. "I think the problem here is that we don't know each other well enough. Though we have explored each other's bodies so thoroughly," he laughed when he felt the heat in her cheeks as he held her face in his hands, "we don't know our minds all that well. Would you like to wait before we consummate our marriage?"

Hemangini sighed. Her husband was being too reasonable and extremely patient. And she knew for a fact how much he desired her. But she liked what he suggested. All this long, they had always had to meet in secret. Now, being man and wife, there was no need for secrecy. They could spend all the time they wanted together, alone, without the need for maids or guards to escort them. It would be a good thing that they would have time to get to know one another.

Looking up into his gaze, she gave a nod. "I would like that. I hope you don't mind."

He shook his head, laughing as he whispered into her ear. "Your body already belongs to me. It's your mind I want to woo before I make you completely mine."

Deeply touched, Hemangini buried her face in his chest, her arms around his lean waist. "Thank you for understanding."

"Shall we return to the chamber?" he asked, kissing her forehead.

"Deven… is there a guest bedroom in your suite?"

"Why?" He lifted his head to look down at her, glad that she was not calling him by his full name now.

"For me. I need a place to sleep."

"You are my wife and you will sleep with me in my chamber. You can rest easy that I will not claim my conjugal rights. We will make love only on the day you are ready and tell me so. Is that clear?"

Hemangini gave her husband a wary look. He was a kshatriya and would be able to resist her proximity, maybe. She wasn't too sure about herself. After all, her body craved him like a bee craved honey.

"What now?" he asked, watching her face keenly, almost able to read the thoughts churning through her mind even as her expression changed, totally fascinated by it.

"Are you sure? About us sleeping in the same bed?" she asked, her voice a shy whisper, even as her gaze clung to his desperately.

"I am absolutely sure. Why? Aren't you?"

Refusing to reply, she buried her face in his chest once again. It was enough that she had got the worry off her chest and handed it over to the man she loved. And he had taken it in his stride. She snuggled closer, feeling much lighter.

Devendra lifted her into his arms and carried her to his chamber. He would somehow convince Hemangini that she was the only woman for him even if it took their whole lives.

"I love you, my princess." Hemangini shivered when he whispered softly into her ear as he placed her on one side of the bed.

18

The Morning After

T he sun was already riding high in the sky when Hemangini opened her eyes. She stretched her arms above her head or tried to, startled at the weight which pressed down her body against the bed. Opening her eyes wide, she looked down, only to find Devendra's face buried in her breasts, his dark curls dishevelled. What was he doing, lying on her chest? Hadn't they agreed to get to know one another better before consummating their wedding?

Of their own accord, her hands ran through the curls which were the texture of raw silk. She breathed deeply, her mind spinning as the subtle aroma of sandalwood oil touched her nostrils. Trailing one hand over his muscular shoulder, she could feel his even breathing as his body rose and fell against her.

Suddenly, she felt him move, the prince's thick moustache brushing over the swell of her breast as he turned his head. "Deven…" Hemangini called to him in a soft whisper.

"Mmm…" He buried his face deeper into her breasts, his arms tightening around her.

That's when Hemangini realised that the knot of her bustier was loose and the upper half of her chest uncovered, her skin responding with fervour to the brush of his face, even as her nipples hardened into pebbles.

"Deven, wake up," she called out again in a louder voice. She was too conscious of the weight of his head on her breasts and couldn't help the feeling of hot desire building deep within the core of her body.

How she wanted him to make love to her! But no, that cannot happen until the time she could be sure that he wouldn't fall for another woman. With a deep sigh of regret shuddering through her body, Hemangini placed a hand on his hard shoulder and shook him. "Wake up Deven."

He opened his eyes in a slit and looked up at her, a smile slowly spreading on his face. "Good morning, my love!"

Colour rushed to Hemangini's face when she noticed the languorous desire in his gaze which heated up her blood. "Good morning!" she responded in a whisper, her throat choking up even as her heartbeat increased to an enormous speed.

"Didn't we agree not to make love for some time? Till I woo your mind?" he asked lazily, his hands caressing her bare waist, making her shiver in delight.

"Mmm."

"Then why are you holding me so close to your tempting body? Is it supposed to be some kind of a challenge? A test of the control I have over mine?" he asked, his voice shaking with laughter even as his eyes teased her mercilessly.

"Deven!" Hemangini tried to glare at him, her attempt quite unsuccessful even as her lavender gaze ran over his handsome features. The shadow of beard on his cheeks only made him appear more masculine and even more attractive than ever. Curiously, she reached a hand to rub her palm over his cheek, finding the rasping sensation beyond delicious.

"Tch tch!" He shook his head at her. "That is not fair, my princess. You can't tempt me so."

"Why can't I?" she asked, slipping into the game he was playing. With her other hand she caressed his right cheek before holding his face between her palms and lifting a challenging brow at him.

"Because it makes me want to kiss you." He bent down to brush his mouth over her luscious lips, once, twice and thrice. Just brushed his mouth, without opening it, thrilled to see the frustration building in her gaze.

"So, why don't you kiss me?" she asked, gripping his face firmly to hold it in front of her before pressing her mouth to his and stroking her tongue firmly over the shape of his masculine lips.

"Hema…" Devendra groaned, opening his mouth to capture her tongue and drawing it deep within, even as he pushed his tongue into hers.

With a soft moan, she gave in to his passionate kiss, revelling in his hold. Taking his hand in hers, she placed it over her breast.

Devendra gave a shudder before removing his mouth from hers and lifted his head to look down at her. He was sorely tempted to touch her breasts and make love to her completely. But he was honour bound to keep his promise to her to woo her mind before he made her totally his. And not only that, he had to convince her that he loved her, and only her. There would never be another woman for him, not in this life. "No, my love. You forget what we agreed upon last night. You don't want me to give in to temptation, do you? Not until you can trust me completely." He gave her a penetrating look, as if to let her know that it was all up to her.

With a sigh, Hemangini turned her head to the side, not keen for him to notice her disappointment. But he had a valid point and she was glad that he had reminded her of it at the right time. Oh, the temptation of the flesh! It was an effort to simply not give in to it and go with the flow. But no, she didn't want to rush into something she might come to regret later. As it is, she loved her husband, a lot. She was bound to only fall more in love with him when they consummated their marriage; and her affection would only increase even more if she gave birth to his child as a result. Her world would come crashing if he fell for another woman after all that.

It did make sense waiting to know more of the man she had married; and know for sure whether he would be loyal only to her during this lifetime.

With a deep sigh, she pushed him away. Surprisingly, it wasn't too difficult as the prince quickly moved to one side. Hiding her disappointment, the princess got out of bed to walk towards the washroom that was in a smaller building behind their quarters.

Devendra lay against the pillows, watching her go, a deep sigh shuddering through his body. He would woo her even if it killed him, hoping that he lived long enough to savour a life with her. He shook his head to himself, a soft smile on his face. Yes, it wouldn't be easy, especially as he could feel his aroused manhood protesting painfully. Yes, it was going to take a long time. But convince her he will, of his loyalty and love towards her, only her.

But even the Prince of Indrapuri didn't expect it would take so long…

The Wooing of the Mind

Indrapuri, towards the end of 1482 AD…

ven Prince Devendra didn't know that it would take so long to woo his wife as a whole year passed by; spending most of his waking hours with his princess. She travelled with him wherever he went, and he insisted that she spend every night in his bed.

And there were kisses, so many of them, much to Hemangini's delight. They talked a lot, Devendra telling her stories about his childhood even as she shared all her dreams with him.

The two of them practised their swashbuckling skills once every week; Devendra totally enamoured by his wife's reflexes and nimble footing.

"Don't you dare let me win," she had threatened him the first time.

"I'm not so foolish as to allow an expert to win without making the challenge worthwhile," he had laughed, parrying her thrust effortlessly.

Riding was their favourite pastime as they raced over plains and climbed over hills morning after morning, finding quiet places to simply sit back and have a heart-to-heart dialogue.

There was a waterfall to the east of the city, dropping down from the mountainside to form a cool glade in a clearing amidst an orchard of trees laden with oranges. It was a lovely setting with many coloured birds twittering over the trees as they fed their young.

There were even a few rabbits and deer that came for a drink at the pool. This was where Devendra taught his wife how to swim.

At her home in Mahendrapuri, Hemangini used to bathe every morning in a shallow pool that had been constructed at the back of her chambers. It had been deep enough for her to float in or just sit back, but not big enough to swim in.

When they reached the area, they tied their horses' reins around trees, letting them graze on the luscious grass in the shadow of the trees. "Would you like to go for a swim?" asked Devendra, taking Hemangini's hand in his.

She looked longingly at the water before saying, "I would love to. But I don't know how."

"I can teach you," he offered, giving her a smile. "You might be more comfortable if you wear your *antariya* above your knees. Can you manage to retie it?" he asked. She will also have to leave her *uttariya* back on the shore. Heat kicked into his body, arousing him painfully as he eyed her. Her silk bustier was bound to get wet and will probably turn transparent. Saliva pooled in his mouth at the thought. "I can help you if you want."

"I think I can manage."

"Give me your *uttariya*," he said, taking it from her when she handed it to him, his eyes on her heaving breasts contained in the bustier.

She walked behind a large tree trunk and retied the folds of her *antariya* tightly so that it left her knees and calves bare. Her cheeks heating up, she stepped out from behind the tree to walk hesitantly towards her husband.

Devendra couldn't lift his gaze above her slender legs which were the colour of rich ivory. Simply beautiful.

The princess in turn stared at her husband with a startled gaze. He had done away with his breeches and tunic and… what was that? Her eyes went round when she noticed that he had used her *uttariya* to wrap it around his lower body, just about covering his manhood. His muscular legs appeared sturdy like the tree trunks around them. It was not as if she hadn't seen his bared body before. But that had been in the lamp light and he had been holding her close at that time, curtailing her view to some extent. Just now, he was standing a few feet away from her, his legs apart, his bearing straight. She couldn't help but feast her eyes on his wide shoulders and chest that narrowed down to a lean waist. Hemangini realised that while her *uttariya* covered him from her sight, it didn't stop her from noticing his tumescent shape, making her colour all the more.

She felt a sudden urge to tear the piece of cloth from him and gaze at him in all his naked glory. With a sigh, she stepped forward, burying her thoughts deep within, completely unaware that her husband could study her expressive face only too easily.

Not uttering a word regarding his observations, the prince said, "Come! The water will be cold," he warned as they stepped into the shallow end.

She gripped his hand tightly, a moan of delight escaping her lips when the cool water lapped around her ankles. It felt so good.

When they reached an area where the water rose up to her waist, the princess turned to face her husband as if to ask, *What now?*

He lifted her up in his arms and laid her face down over the water surface, placing a firm hand under her stomach to keep her afloat. "It is not too difficult," said Devendra, as he showed her how to use her arms and legs to propel herself in the water.

A visibly excited Hemangini followed his instructions carefully and it wasn't long before she took a turn around the circular pool under Devendra's guidance. It was one of the most exhilarating experiences of her life.

It was much later when they dried themselves on a rock, Hemangini tilting her head to the sunshine as she leaned her hands on the rock at the back, her legs stretched out even as her upper body was thrust forward.

Devendra sat next to her, his eyes on her chest, her darkened nipples tempting him through the silk cloth that had turned transparent with wetness. It was both pleasure and torture as he watched the cloth drying little by little in the sunlight.

I hope I don't turn impotent due to abstinence by the time my dear wife agrees to bed me. He laughed at the thought that sprang into his mind.

Hemangini turned her head to look at her laughing husband. "What's the matter?" she asked curiously.

He shook his head. "You may not think it a laughing matter."

"Why don't you allow me to decide for myself?" she asked, sitting up straight.

He told her and he was right. Hemangini didn't find the matter humorous, not at all.

"I… I don't know what to say," she said, her voice apologetic. "I need more time. I…"

He reached across to lay his hand over her mouth, shaking his head. "I was only jesting. You take all the time you want."

"You make me fall in love with you more and more," she said in a whisper, kissing his palm.

After the first visit, they went to the pool often, Hemangini loving the activity as with each visit, she got better and better at swimming, soon able to keep up with Devendra's pace.

She accompanied her husband when he went hunting; and they also sat through the court sessions that King Chandrabhan held as they studied the manner in which he dealt with the citizens' petitions.

A visit to the market was a weekly affair, Devendra speaking personally to every shopkeeper and ensuring they had a good trade and also making sure they received enough income to lead a comfortable life with their families.

All the children of the kingdom were sent to the Gurukul; even the girls. "Education is a must for everyone, till the age of sixteen. They don't just learn to read and write but also learn one vocational skill, anything of their choice."

Hemangini was impressed with the way Prince Devendra interacted with the people of Indrapuri, with his heart.

He was patience personified, not once pushing her into having a physical relationship with him. The princess, who had to rein in her passion many a time, still enjoyed the slow pace at which he romanced her, keeping his focus completely on her. She was aware that he was probably having a difficult time curbing his own ardour, and truly appreciated his gesture. Not once, by word or deed, did Devendra show the frustration that he must be surely undergoing and she adored him for it. After all, a marriage was the mating of minds more than bodies. She didn't want their relationship to fade out after the fervour of making love dimmed over time.

One day, a little more than a year after they had been married, King Chandrabhan announced that he was going to travel around the kingdom, checking on the welfare of his people.

"Would you like us to accompany my father on his trip around Indrapuri?" asked Devendra, holding his wife in his lap, his arms around her waist. It was late in the night and they were sitting on the veranda at the back of their chamber, facing the garden.

Leaning back on his chest, Hemangini asked, "Will we be riding on horses?" Her heart picked up speed as she thought of travelling to new places and meeting strangers. It would be so wonderful, especially at Devendra's side.

"Ideally yes. Unless you want to go by chariot. There won't be too many of us; about six, I think. That's the only way to travel fast."

"Won't Kalpana and Kamini be able to go with us? At least one of them?"

His lips stretched in a mischievous smile as he pressed his chin into the curve of her shoulder, his breath teasing the tendrils of hair that had escaped her knot. "I can be of service," he offered.

Her heart jumped to her throat, her volatile imagination going wild as she visualised him tying a bustier around her breasts or wrapping her *antariya* around her legs. Will he be able to deal with her long hair and style it, day after day? Her excitement knew no bounds.

"What? You don't think I can handle it? I can even help wash your back during your bath," he said teasingly, kissing her cheek.

She turned her head to give him an adoring look, her lips pouting. "As long as you allow me to return the favour. I am sure your valet won't be accompanying us either."

Devendra gave her a nod, grinning. That Sanjaya might disown the prince was another matter. But if Hemangini's maid could not go, then the prince's valet could not accompany them either. "Then, shall I tell Father that the two of us will go with him?"

"Yes, please. I would love to see all of your kingdom."

"Our kingdom," said the prince, crushing her to his hard frame. He ignored his protesting body. His only aim right now was to gain his wife's complete trust.

On the Way Back Home

Indrapuri, 1483 AD

They were just about half a day away from the capital of Indrapuri when the king's party stopped for the night at the small but luxuriously appointed establishment that belonged to the king. The king's ancestors had built many such structures in all directions around the kingdom for the royal family's use while travelling. A pair of caretakers, a man and his wife, kept the place clean and ready for occupation at all times.

The cook who had been travelling with them had made a delicious dinner consisting of three courses. Being the only woman in the group, Hemangini had the option of dining in her chamber. But more than eager to remain with her husband, she sat with the others as they relished the freshly caught fish cooked in a spicy sauce along with steamed rice and deliciously sautéed potatoes.

She sat back, sipping from a wooden mug, the herbal tea the cook had prepared at her instigation. After all, Hemangini wasn't keen on drinking *madira* with every meal like the others did.

"We will be home by tomorrow evening." Devendra spoke to her in a soft voice.

"Hmm." Feeling a sudden rush of melancholy, the princess realised that she might have to share her husband's attention with the rest of his family in the palace. And she didn't care for that at all. While they had spent a lot of time together, he did give a portion of it to his mother and the others every day before they took off on this journey. Going around the countryside with the small group, Hemangini had been only too thrilled that she had her husband's complete attention to herself as the king and the others had their own agenda. The two of them could have been travelling alone for all the attention the others paid them. It had been just perfect.

But tomorrow… Hemangini sighed. A sudden thought struck her. *Am I being too selfish thinking only of myself?* Devendra had kept his promise to not make love to her. And he had also done his best to win her heart. How much more did she need to be convinced of his loyalty?

She turned her head to gaze into his eyes, running the tip of her tongue over her suddenly dry lips.

He lifted an eyebrow in query.

She gave a small nod towards their room, not keen to be the first one to leave the dining hall; not before the king did.

Thinking that she must be tired, Devendra gave her a nod of understanding before turning to his father. "Shall we take your leave, *Pitashri*?"

King Chandrabhan, who was drinking from his wine cup, turned to look at his son and gave a smile. "Go on, my children. I will see you both in the morning. And Hema, my dear, I must say it has been a pleasure travelling with you. Not one woman I know can make for such a calm travel companion. I must say that Deven is very lucky to have you for his wife."

"*Pitashri!*" Hemangini bowed her head, truly touched by the king's words. "I am honoured. I wish you a very good night."

Devendra took her hand, leading her to their room. He couldn't help thinking that his wife appeared so beautiful even while sporting the simplest of garments, in cotton, most of the time, and very few pieces of jewellery. After all, they hadn't wanted to carry too many silk garments or jewellery during the rigorous excursion.

"You get ready for bed, my princess. I will take a walk and return soon."

"Deven!" Hemangini placed a hand on his arm, stopping him in his tracks. She had come to a decision. She wanted to give herself fully to her husband, the man she loved, the one who loved her unconditionally. "Stay with me."

"Naturally! I will return soon."

She shook her head, refusing to let go of his arm, her nails digging into the muscle. "Don't go."

"Hema, I…"

She let go of his arm to place a hand over his mouth, moving closer to press her aroused body to his. "I love you."

"I love you too, Hema. But…"

"Not with just my body, Deven," she interrupted him to say in a heated whisper, "but with my mind too. Will you make love to me?"

Devendra groaned in capitulation, gathering her into his arms in a crushing grip before bending down to kiss her on her mouth. He lifted her in his arms without breaking the kiss as he carried her to the bed and placed her on it, lying down beside her.

She returned his kiss with equal fervour, her fingers clutching his tunic as she tried to remove it from his body, eager to touch his naked flesh. All those times she had washed his back while they bathed in lakes and rivers during the travel, her palms and fingers had tingled with desire. She pulled his head down to hers and spoke into his ear, "I am sorry I made you wait this long. I…"

He shook his head, tasting her lower lip with his tongue before biting it gently. "Do you believe me when I say that you are the only woman for me?" he asked.

"Yes, I do. Please forgive my…"

He stopped her effectively by kissing her deeply. "There is no need to apologise, my love. I am glad that I have your complete trust now. The wait was truly worth it."

"You, my Deven, are truly patient," she said, overwhelmed by his words. Turning around, she offered her back to him. "Will you untie my bustier, please?"

"Are you begging me, my princess?" Devendra's voice shook with laughter as he untied the knot behind her back, letting the cloth slip down as he reached out with his hands to cup her breasts from behind.

Her answering giggle turned into a moan, "Aah!" She sank back into his chest, adoring his hands on her person as he squeezed her twin mounds in his large hands. "I have craved your touch, my prince," declared the passionate princess, holding on to his muscular arms even as she thrust her body closer into his hands.

"As I have craved to touch you. And I can't wait to touch your core, my love. Do you remember the last time? You were so hot and wet."

Hemangini moaned some more as she recalled that night almost fourteen months ago when he had pleasured her with his fingers and tongue. "Only for you, my prince." She turned her head sideways to rub her cheek on his shoulder. "Will you take your tunic off?" she demanded impatiently.

Devendra let go of her breasts with reluctance; pulling the tunic over his head and throwing it aside before gathering her once again in his arms.

Hemangini turned around to wrap her arms tightly around his lean waist, rubbing her breasts against his muscular chest that was sprinkled with crisp hair. "That feels so lovely," she growled, taking a bite of his shoulder.

"Vixen!" He growled right back, rubbing his hands over her silky back, even as he unhooked the slim gold *kamarbandh* which held her *antariya* in place.

"You know that day at the glade in the orchard, the first time you took me swimming?"

"Hmm." Devendra took a small bite of the plump breast he held in his palm, making her quiver with pleasure.

"You looked so beautiful using my *uttariya* to cover your loins," she continued, lifting her breast with a hand to feed the nipple into his eager mouth, moaning loudly when he suckled on it greedily.

Even as he feasted on her breast, Devendra looked into her lavender gaze, an eyebrow raised, encouraging her to continue with her story.

Her hands caressing his locks of hair that so reminded her of raw silk, she pulled his head closer to her body, saying, "I want to see you, your manhood, without any clothing."

Removing his mouth from her nipple swollen with his kisses, Devendra smiled at her, colour running up his lean cheeks, saying, "Anything for you, my princess." Letting go of her, he stepped down from the bed and removed the knot at his waist before pushing down his breeches.

Hemangini protested when he bent down to completely remove his breeches when she couldn't see his lower body.

Laughing, he stepped out of his breeches to stand straight and tall in front of her, his tumescent shaft swinging free to draw her fascinated gaze.

Hemangini leaned back on the bedhead, her hands behind her back, her breasts thrust out proudly as she eyed her husband's muscular body, her gaze clinging to his manhood. "God in heaven! Deven! You have the most magnificent body!" Her voice was thick with longing as she leaned forward to touch him, laughing when she felt his shaft convulse in response. Going on her knees, she clasped both her hands around his manhood and caressed him from the root to the tip.

"You feel so wonderful and hard; like an iron rod sheathed in velvet."

He pushed her back on the bed to swiftly unwrap her *antariya* before lying down next to her, not at all averse to it when she refused to let go of him. He traced a path from her forehead down the side of her face to her neck with his tongue, pausing at the pulsing vein at the juncture of her neck and shoulder, stroking it rhythmically, smiling at her gasps of pleasure. "You look so beautiful, my love," he told her in a whisper as he moved down further to kiss her breasts.

Letting go of his shaft, she clutched his head close to her chest, her whole body trembling with need when she felt his mouth close on a breast. "Deven..."

He turned his head to suckle the other breast, taking the nipple between his teeth and biting it gently, laughing when she sprang from the bed, like an arrow released from a bow. He stroked his hand down her abdomen before he ventured towards the curls between her thighs.

"Deven..." she moaned when she felt his caress against her feminine mound, her legs thrashing impatiently.

Immersing a long finger into her core, he pleasured her as he moved it in and out, in and out, his gaze on her flushed face and half-closed eyes. "Do you like it, my love?" he asked, bending down to kiss a corner of her mouth.

"I want more. You finger is not enough..." She opened heavy eyelids to look into his gaze as she implored him, even as she traced a finger around a flat male nipple, fascinated to see it beading tightly right in front of her eyes. She lifted her face to kiss him there, stroking his nipple with her tongue.

Devendra groaned as he pushed her down on the bed to climb over her and settle down between her legs. Placing his hands on her slender thighs, he moved her legs apart, bending them gently at the knees before he moved his shaft towards her core. Gritting his teeth to hold himself back, careful to not hurt her, he pushed within slowly.

Hemangini grew impatient as she clutched his shoulders tightly, her nails digging into his flesh even as she pushed her lower body closer to him.

"Patience, my love," he said, his jaw clenched with the control he was exercising over his aching shaft.

"No, Deven. I don't want to be patient, not anymore," said the princess, too eager for their joining as she pressed her mouth to his and thrust her tongue deeply into it.

Losing control, Devendra groaned as he pushed deeper into her, swallowing the muffled sound of her pain as he stilled within her, waiting for her body to adjust to his size.

"Deven..." she punched him on his shoulder as she looked deeply into his eyes, a smile in her own. "I like this better than your finger," declared the passionate princess.

Devendra gave a startled laugh, responding to the restless thrashing of her legs as he pulled out of her core before pushing in once again. Soon, he was riding his wife, her long drawn out moans music to his ears as he sought to give her satisfaction before finding his own.

Holding on to his shoulders, Hemangini met him thrust for thrust, a pressure building deep within her womb. She craved for that elusive something which seemed within sight but just out of her reach as she felt him move faster and faster, even as he bent down to run his tongue over a turgid nipple. The next moment, she felt as if both thunder and lightning had struck her at the juncture of her thighs as she climaxed, a long moan issuing from her lips as she raked her nails down his back. "Deven…"

The prince groaned at his own release, glad that he could hold back until he had given her the gratification she sought. "My love…" He tried to move to the side, only she wouldn't let him go before he fell over her supine figure, doing his best not to hurt her with his hard muscles.

She held on to him tightly, her arms wrapped around him, her legs crossed as she continued to hold his softened shaft within her. "You are mine and I refuse to let you go," declared his princess.

He grinned at her, too breathless to give her a reply as he buried his face in her breasts.

The Queen's Shock

Kalpana met a visibly excited princess, her own face tight with tension. Kamini had an equally grim expression on her face when she greeted her mistress.

"How was your journey, My Lady?" asked Kalpana, washing the princess's back as she sat in a large, round brass tub filled with hot water.

"It was wonderful," said the princess as she gazed dreamily at the carved ceiling of her dressing room.

Both the maids looked at each other, wondering how to disclose the message to the princess, the one Kalpana had received from Queen Kanchana Devi's maid Ratnamala.

Kamini brought a brass incense burner with glowing coals before adding some powdered incense to it. Heavy and aromatic smoke rose from the burner which the maid placed under a round cane basket before spreading the length of the princess's hair over it.

"My Lady!" Kalpana hesitated to say more than that.

Hemangini, who was sitting on the carpet to facilitate the drying of her hair with incense smoke, looked up at her maid who was wringing her hands, an anxious expression on her face. "What is it, Kalpana? Is something wrong?" she asked, the smile refusing to leave her face as she recalled Devendra's passionate lovemaking in the early hours of that very morning, before they left to return home.

"Er... My Lady! I don't like to gossip, but..." Kalpana paused again. It wasn't as if she was afraid of her mistress whom she had known from the time when they had been children. But she didn't want to hurt her and what she was going to say would definitely bring distress to Princess Hemangini.

Growing impatient, Hemangini snapped her fingers at Kalpana. "Enough now, Kalpana. Tell me what is bothering you," she commanded.

"You know Ratnamala, the Rani Maa's maid?" she asked in a quavering voice.

Hemangini gave a nod even as a frown pleated her eyebrows. She didn't want to hear anything about Queen Kanchana Devi or her maid. While she would always behave respectfully towards Devendra's mother, the truth was that she didn't like her mother-in-law.

"Ratnamala told me that the royal astrologer had visited the Rani Maa as she wanted him to read your horoscope." She paused when she noticed the deepening frown on Hemangini's face before continuing in a rush, "I believe the astrologer said that you were barren." Kalpana choked, bending down to look at the floor even as a dark flush rose from her neck all the way up to her forehead. She felt so ashamed to bring such a terrible message to the princess.

Hemangini took a deep breath as she calmed down the temper that rose up from within her. Alright! The astrologer had declared that she was barren. What of it? "So what?" asked the princess.

Kamini continued from where Kalpana had left off. "So, the Rani Maa plans to find the prince another wife."

Hemangini stared at her maids, her mouth wide open as she listened to Kamini's words with deep shock. Isn't this what she had been worried about? Isn't this the reason why she had not let her husband make love to her all this long? Only last night she had concluded that he loved her and only her. And she had given herself to him believing that. It had not even been one whole day and already his mother was planning to find him another wife.

The princess didn't know if she should be angry with Queen Kanchana Devi or her husband. Even if his mother told him to marry again, why should he agree to it? Hemangini fumed, her face red with temper as she allowed the maids to deck her up, not at all interested in either the clothes she wore or the jewellery. After the month of journeying, she realised that while she loved wearing finery; silk clothes and diamond jewellery were not the primary concerns of her life.

Once she was ready, she walked out of the dressing room, not even aware when the two maids went along with her. Just when she would have stepped into their bedchamber to speak to her husband, Sanjaya met her at the door.

"My Lady!" He bowed his head to the princess. "Prince Devendra has gone to meet the queen who had sent word for him. He left a message that My Lady should directly join the family in the dining hall."

Glaring at him as if it was all his mistake, Hemangini turned abruptly and walked across the royal garden towards the main palace.

"My Lady!" Kalpana placed a hand on the princess's arm to stop her in her tracks.

"What?" Hemangini scowled at her maid. "Can't you see that I am in a hurry?" she snarled. Her heart was beating heavily in her chest as she wondered what poison the queen was filling her son's mind with. It was obvious that the older woman didn't like her daughter-in-law.

"Please forgive me, My Lady! It's just that I think you should calm down before you go ahead."

"I agree with Kalpana, My Lady." Kamini joined in the conversation when she realised that her mistress was finally in a state to listen to them. "The situation calls for strategy, not direct attack."

The frown receded from Hemangini's forehead as she looked at her friends. "What do you suggest?" she asked earnestly. By now, she was tired of fighting her roiling emotions. She loved the prince and wanted him for herself.

"We should understand that this is not the prince's fault," said Kalpana, looking at her mistress shrewdly. She realised that Hemangini was hurt that he might want to take another spouse.

"He had been travelling with you when the astrologer visited the queen. Any decision of another marriage was made by the queen and must have had nothing to do with Prince Devendra." Kamini added her views.

Hemangini sagged against a mango tree, her breath releasing in a deep sigh. What they said made sense. This was not at all Devendra's fault. He probably wasn't even aware that his mother had taken the call of getting him another wife. As for the astrologer saying that she was barren; Hemangini was not too impressed. The man could be wrong for all they knew. At eighteen, it was too early to know if she was barren or not. And well, the others did not know that the prince and his wife had consummated their wedding only the earlier night. She rubbed her cheeks as colour rushed to her face as her mind went over last night.

Straightening her shoulders, she started walking slowly and gracefully towards the main palace, speaking to her maids as they continued on their way to the dining hall. "I am going to pretend that you never said anything to me," she told Kalpana.

The maids grinned their approval. "I think that would be perfect," said Kalpana, pleased with her mistress's decision.

"You wanted to see me, Mother?" Devendra asked as he stepped into Queen Kanchana Devi's chamber.

"Ratna, you may leave us alone." The queen waited for her maid to go before turning to her son with a wide smile. She placed a hand on his head when he bent down to touch her feet. "*Aayushmaan bhava!*" she blessed him with a long life.

"How have you been, Mother?" he asked, sitting down next to her on the ornately carved and cushioned chair for two.

"Old age is catching up on me. What else?" she said, the look of a sacrificial lamb on her face. In a sudden change of mood, the queen placed a hand on Devendra's shoulder, giving him an adoring smile. "You look tired, my son," she said, not at all impressed with the glow on his face. The truth was that he appeared revitalised. But she wasn't going to acknowledge it.

He shrugged. "I don't know, Mother. I don't feel tired at all."

"How was your excursion? Did you get to meet many of our citizens?" she asked.

Devendra didn't admit that it was the king who had met his people. Whereas he and his princess had treated the whole excursion as a holiday. He simply gave her a nod. "Did you have something specific to tell me in private, Mother?" The messenger she had sent over earlier had asked the prince to meet her in private before the family dinner.

"Yes, Deven." The queen gave a dramatic sigh. The Devendra she knew had always listened to her, following her advice. But that had been before he married the Princess of Mahendrapuri. Like a typical mother-in-law, Kanchana Devi was convinced that her son had completely changed after the younger woman had entered his life. Deep down, she was jealous of Hemangini's position in her son's life. Which is exactly why she wanted him to marry again. After all, if King Chandrabhan could marry four wives, Devendra could marry at least two. "It has been fourteen months since your wedding to Hemangini."

He nodded. "You are right, Mother." He bit his lip to stop the smile that sprang to his lips. He knew how much time had passed after the wedding. After all, it had been he who had been waiting all this long to have the marriage consummated.

"It's been a long while. Shouldn't Hemangini be with child by now?" she asked, looking at her son cunningly.

How could it even be possible if she hadn't had a physical relationship with her husband during the fourteen months? Devendra thought to himself, amused. But he didn't mention all that to his mother. "We both are young, mother. It will happen in time."

"No, Devendra, I don't agree with you. You are forgetting that you are the Crown Prince of Indrapuri and it's your duty to produce an heir to the throne for the next generation. How can you be so relaxed about it?" she asked in a scolding voice.

"I think that more than my being relaxed, you are being overanxious about this, Mother. Why don't you give us some more time?" he asked in a pacifying tone, taking her hands in his.

Sparks flew out of the queen's fiery gaze. "Time for what? How long does it take to give birth to a child? Don't be a fool, Deven. You don't want Gagandeep to wed some princess and father a child before you do. If that happens…"

"Gagandeep's son will become the heir to the throne. So, what if that happens, Mother? Gagan is also my father's son. Why shouldn't his child become the king after me?"

Queen Kanchana Devi sprang up from the chair to stand in front of her son, her fisted hands on her hips as she glared at the crown prince. "I know you are foolish. But even I did not expect you to be so stupid. Who gives up a throne for the sake of his step-brother's unborn child? Gagandeep is not even married. How could you…?"

Devendra gave his mother a serene smile, unaware that instead of calming her, it only managed to inflame her temper all the more. "Mother, it wasn't I who suggested that he might get married and produce a son before I did. Why are we arguing, Mother? Be a little patient and we—Hemangini and I—will give you the grandson you seek."

She lifted a hand in front of her face as if to stop him from continuing. "I don't think Hemangini would deliver a child, ever. I have consulted with Astrologer Agnimitra. He checked her horoscope and says that she is barren."

It was Devendra's turn to lose his temper. He got up to stand straight and tall in front of his mother. "I will have the astrologer thrown in prison for spreading a rumour such as this. I am going to send the guards to put the man in chains and drag him to the palace right now." He turned to walk towards the entrance to the chamber, fuming with temper.

Queen Kanchana Devi was shaken by her son's temper. She never knew he had one. Always calm and serene, Devendra personified patience, at least to his mother. Even now, though she knew his anger was aimed at the astrologer, she didn't want the mischief she had made exposed—spreading the word that Hemangini was barren; the astrologer had never said anything like that. Her son might never forgive her if he found out the truth.

"Stop, Deven. And listen to me. Time will tell if Hemangini is capable of bearing a child or not. But I have a better idea. I want you to get married to another woman, as soon as possible. In fact, I have sent messengers to three different kingdoms, seeking their princesses' hands in marriage for you. You can choose from one of them or maybe even marry all of them. This is my final decision."

So! It was nothing to do with the astrologer. While he loved his mother, Devendra was well aware of her mischief-making nature. Queen Kanchana Devi didn't like the other queens and had never made the effort to get along with them. Now, it looked like she didn't like Hemangini either. He hoped that his wife was different. The prince wanted peace to reign in his family.

"Listen, Mother," he said in a soft but firm voice, placing his hands on the queen's shoulders. "Hemangini is the only wife for me whether she delivers a son or a daughter or no child at all. I will never marry a second time. And that is *my* final decision. I will see you at dinner, Mother." He walked out of the queen's chamber, not waiting for her reply or he would have noticed his mother's jaw drop open, as utter shock clouded her face.

EPILOGUE

An Heir is Born

Indrapuri, 1485 AD

Princess Hemangini smiled when she saw her five-month-old daughter giving her father a toothless smile as she lay in his arms. The little Princess Dakshayani appeared so tiny in Devendra's muscular arms as she kicked her legs vigorously even as she tried to curl her hand around Devendra's forefinger.

"She is so beautiful, my love. I can watch her all day long."

Hemangini laughed, placing a hand on her husband's shoulder as she looked down at the babe. "I have to agree with you. She is beautiful and looks a lot like her father."

He turned his gaze to look up at his wife with an adoring gaze. "Does she? I can see your features in hers," he insisted, turning to his child to touch her tiny nose.

Dakshayani gurgled at her parents, lifting her arms towards her mother when she saw her.

"She must be hungry," said Hemangini, taking the child in her arms to go sit on the bed. "Deven, will you help me untie my bustier?" she asked her husband.

Giving her a mischievous grin, he loosened the tie and watched his daughter close her little mouth over a nipple greedily.

"She does not cry when she is hungry, our Dakshayani. She must have really taken after her mother." He had been impressed by the way Hemangini dealt with his mother, courageously.

The princess always treated the queen with respect, but did exactly what she believed was right. In the past two years, the princess had brought about a number of changes in the kingdom for the betterment of the people. She had personally seen to it that every cottage in the kingdom was repaired, ensuring that there were no leaking roofs. More wells were dug to make sure everyone was provided with water not far from their homes. She had even sat during meetings with traders and had brought forth a number of reforms.

"I have an idea," said the prince, leaning forward to kiss her breast.

Hemangini gave a soft sigh, lifting a hand to pull his head closer. "Hmm…" Her whole body shivered with longing. It had been two years since they first made love. But she simply couldn't have enough of her prince. It looked like he had captured both her mind and body completely.

Taking a gentle bite of her tender flesh, he asked, "Would you like us to have a son?" giving her a wicked grin.

"What if it is another daughter?" she lifted her chin to challenge him.

"Which is the idea I was going to speak to you about before you distracted me. I am thinking of declaring Dakshayani my heir. So, what if she is a girl? If she is anything like her mother, she will make a great ruler."

Tears shimmered in Hemangini's eyes as she gave her husband an adoring look, not noticing that her daughter had fallen asleep in her arms, her little mouth wide open.

Devendra gently removed the child from her mother's lap, the back of his hand brushing against the sensitised nipple, making Hemangini gasp. Giving her a wink, he placed Dakshayani in the cradle, wrapping a soft cloth around her, before turning to his wife.

Gathering her in his arms, he bent down to draw his tongue over the exposed nipple, thrilled to hear his wife's moan of delight. "What do you say?"

"About what?" asked the thoroughly distracted Hemangini as he crushed her to his chest. She couldn't wait to make love to her husband.

Pushing her back on the bed, Devendra lay next to her, saying, "About declaring Dakshayani my heir."

"I like the idea. But what will the king and queen say?"

"You know my father is already Dakshayani's slave. I am sure he will look at it with an open mind. It isn't as if queens haven't ruled over kingdoms before now." Devendra didn't say anything about his mother. Kanchana Devi was an unhappy woman and there was no solution to that. She had been terribly upset when Hemangini delivered a girl instead of the boy the queen had been hoping for. She had even suggested that Devendra should consider getting married again.

While Devendra hadn't confided in his wife regarding his mother's suggestion—both times—Hemangini was aware of what the queen wanted. After all, Ratnamala made it a point to speak about it to Kalpana. What really thrilled the princess was that her husband simply wasn't interested.

Well, where would he find the time and energy after keeping his wife satisfied in bed?

Hemangini sighed when he brushed his moustache across the sensitive tips of her breasts. Without even getting up from her supine position, she expertly untied the knot of his breeches, pushing them down his muscular thighs before taking his thick shaft in her hand.

His gaze heating with desire, he moved between her legs to push his manhood within her core before beginning yet another dance of life they performed night after night.

Devendra knew that he must be the happiest man in the kingdom, one who was married to the passionate princess.

THE END

MORE BOOKS
BY
SUNDARI
VENKATRAMAN

SUNDARI
VENKATRAMAN
AMAZON BESTSELLING AUTHOR
THE Rebel PRINCESS
THE PRINCESS SERIES BOOK 2

Book #2 from The Princess Series
THE REBEL PRINCESS

Having lost her royal parents in a palace fire at the young age of four, Chamundeswari is brought up to be the docile princess of a vassal kingdom by her stepmother who is also the newly crowned queen and her brother, the chief minister.

Though Vijayendran is the youngest born of the Chozha Emperor and his temple dancer wife, he grows up to be a great warrior and leader under the auspices of his elder brother Rajendran only after his father's death. He has been especially trained by the newly crowned king to win over territories and annex them to the greatest empire of those times.

The earth quakes and the skies shiver when Chamundeswari and Vijayendran come face to face. But is everything what it appears to be on the surface? Forget being docile, the princess with a tiger for her pet, appears to be a rebel through and through. And the warrior whose strength is to annex regions could be the very person the princess needs to save her kingdom.

But will The Rebel Princess heed the words of the man who sets her on fire with a mere glance?

SUNDARI
VENKATRAMAN
AMAZON BESTSELLING AUTHOR
Once Bitten
TWICE LUCKY

A contemporary romance
by Sundari Venkatraman…
ONCE BITTEN TWICE LUCKY

Deepshika feels as free as a bird once she decides to kick her womaniser husband out of her life. The lawyer is confident of bringing up her teenage kids with her father's help.

Karan isn't all that upset when his wife dumps him, leaving behind their preteen daughter for him to bring up. But the alimony she claims comes as a rude shock.

Sparks fly when the shocked husband meets the divorced, divorce lawyer. But what will happen when their respective children come face to face? Will they accept their parents' relationship or rebel against it?

Will the once bitten Deepshika and Karan be lucky in their relationship the second time?

SUNDARI
VENKATRAMAN
AMAZON BESTSELLING AUTHOR
Tinder
Loving Care

One more contemporary romance
by Sundari Venkatraman…
TINDER LOVING CARE

Sparks fly when Advik Hegde and Aaradhya Iyer meet via the Tinder app.

Advik resists, citing work pressure and targets while the bold career-minded Aaradhya pursues him relentlessly. Unable to resist, he falls into a relationship of sorts with her, without thinking too much of the future…

…until the past comes back to bite them.

And what a past it is! The Iyers and Hegdes don't seem all that different from the Montagues and Capulets of William Shakespeare's Romeo and Juliet.

The first generation fought while the second suffers in silence! Will the Gen-Next also buckle under pressure?

It's a story of Ego versus Heart! Read on to find out which one is the stronger of the two in this eternal tug of war.

Connect with Sundari Venkatraman here:

Sundari Venkatraman Books

Sundari Venkatraman Books

https://www.sundarivenkatraman.in

Author Sundari Venkatraman

@sundarivenkat

@sundarivenkatraman

sundarivenkat@gmail.com